tropes

bakery owner & hockey player

snowed in

best friend's brother

dislike to love

the one who got away

independent eldest daughter

golden retriever caretaker

only one hot tub

Holly's Bakery

📍 MAYFIELD, MA

MAVERICKS

ADLER

68

CALEB ADLER   #68

FORWARD

CONTENTS

ABOUT THE BOOK

Snowed in with the one man I never want to see again? Not my dream holiday vacation.

My charming cabin getaway starts by fending off
a bear attack with my rolling pin.
Except...the bear is actually my best friend's brother. The
star hockey player who stole my heart and broke it.

Thanks, blizzard. Now I'm stuck alone with Caleb.
He's still frustratingly hot, and cocky as ever.

This is what I get for taking time off
from my beloved bakery.
At least there are enough beds...but *only one hot tub.*

Despite the cold, the inescapable heat between us sizzles. For every inch of space I keep from him, he crosses it to make my control unravel.

I can't fall for how tempting he looks chopping firewood to keep us warm. Or how irresistible it is when he takes care of all my problems before I realize them. *Not again.*

Caleb won't wear me down, no matter how hard he tries to convince me I'm the one who got away.

Once the snow clears, we're going separate ways. If he believes this is his second chance to win me back, well...he can *kiss my sugar cookies*.

PLAYLIST

Winter Wonderland — Laufey
Christmas Time Is Here — Tori Kelly
Miss You Most (At Christmas Time) — Mariah Carey
Man I Need — Olivia Dean
Carry You Home — Alex Warren
Close To You — Gracie Abrams
So Easy (To Fall In Love) — Olivia Dean
'tis the damn season — Taylor Swift
Kissing In the Cold - Mistletoe Version — Florrie
Sugar Talking — Sabrina Carpenter
Honey — Taylor Swift
Santa Tell Me — Ariana Grande
A Nonsense Christmas — Sabrina Carpenter
HOMESICK — Mico
Santa Baby — Laufey

PLAYLIST

When Did You Get Hot? — Sabrina Carpenter

back to friends — sombr

December — Ariana Grande

Baby I'm Coming Home — Ally Brooke

Not Just On Christmas — Ariana Grande

Baby I'm Yours — Arctic Monkeys

Winter Song — Leslie Odom Jr., Cynthia Erivo

CHAPTER 1
HOLLY

Hundreds of cookies surround me. Several dozen sugar cookies with a suggestively tongue-in-cheek design occupy every available space, all waiting to become decorated masterpieces too pretty to eat. I'm in my own personal form of heaven.

Seriously, I hope no one overhears the enthusiastic noises I sometimes make without realizing when I'm swept up in the baking zone and dancing around the kitchen.

A girl just loves a sweet treat, okay?

When I inhale the scent of baked goodness, I can't hold back. I should probably turn up the cheery holiday playlist I have on in the background to be safe, or people could get the wrong idea about why I named my shop Blissful Bites Bakery.

It's the most wonderful time of year: Christmas, my favorite.

The season with dazzling lights, cute winter outfits, delicious food meant to be shared with the people in your life, and all the snuggling with my favorite blankets.

The bakery is decked out in festive decor—pink, of course, just like my darling little cottage shop usually is. The cozy atmosphere is more comforting than ever adorned with garlands of dried orange slices, cinnamon sticks, tinsel, and dainty velvet bows dotting the miniature pine trees I put around the space.

In the front of the shop, the pastel counter stretches along the side wall with a display case full of yummy treats of all kinds arranged in baskets and on vintage cake stands I thrifted. A mismatched array of tables, antique loveseats, and the nook by the front window offer customers a comfy place to enjoy the snuggly intimate vibes.

The holiday season is also the busiest time for my custom cookie orders. They're the top-seller I'm best known for after building my baking business online in college. Thanks to the loyal following of my customer base, I was able to open my storefront last year in my dream location on a quaint street of shops in Mayfield, Massachusetts.

My latest creations are spread in batches on every surface of the kitchen while I hum along to the music.

They fill the air with their scrumptious, mouthwatering aromas. As much as I love a scented candle, nothing beats the real deal to delight your senses.

"Oh my god. So many sugary boobs." Leta, one of the new staff members I hired part-time, gapes at the cookies I'm icing on her way in through the back door.

"I know, right?" I laugh as I carefully pipe royal icing.

Before it hardens, I use the fine needle tip of my detailing tool to create a white fluffy edging for the plunging sweetheart neckline on the well-endowed Mrs. Claus busts the customer requested.

"More than I needed to see first thing in the morning," she says.

Admiring my handiwork, I pick up a finished cookie and shimmy it in front of me. "She's so hot in her slutty little red number. Do you think this version of Mrs. Claus calls Santa her Daddy, or is he on his knees begging her to be his Mommy before he peels this off of her?"

Leta whoops with laughter, her shiny dark curls bouncing against her round tan cheeks. Though she's only a handful of years older than me in her early thirties, being around her cheerful personality makes me feel like she's here for me in place of my mom. She swats at me like she's scandalized, but she plays along.

"You deserve to be on the naughty list just for saying that."

"What?" I joke, fanning myself. "You've never thought about it? A big, strong man, well-loved by all, on his knees for you? A girl can dream."

She shakes her head with a fond expression and gestures at me head to toe, from my soft pink hair tied high in a bow to my brightly-colored apron patterned with frosted Christmas tree cakes.

"I never would've guessed someone who looks like a glittery cupcake fairy could have such a dirty mind."

I shrug. "What can I say? I'm as layered as those pretty cakes in the display case. My favorite color is pink, I love the art of baking more than anything in the world, and," I drawl with a giggle, "I'm confidently in tune with my sensual side. Yes, you've heard it here, folks of Mayfield's historic district: women have needs, too, and I, Holly Duncan, am proudly open about being one of them."

Not that I've had those needs met by anyone else, man or woman, lately.

Scratch that.

It's been a long time since I've been with someone other than my battery powered besties tucked away in my nightstand.

"Shh, not so loud," Leta chides. "If Marjorie hears you next door, you'll give her a heart attack."

I scoff with a smile. "Have you not seen the books she stocks in the romance section? Marjorie absolutely knows a good time. I recommend the historical romances if you want something to make you purr."

She busies herself washing up at the sink to prep for her shift. "The same sweet elderly woman who feeds every stray cat in the alley behind the shops and waters the fake flowers in her window boxes?"

"Honestly, she's genius for that. What a great way to overhear the best gossip on the block." I get back to work with a fresh piping bag for the next batch. "I'm telling you, that woman has lived a good life. She's probably got the best stories from her adventures in love. And one of these days? I'm going to get some of them out of her."

The topic of love lives has my thoughts veering down a path I rarely let myself entertain for long. I stop myself before my perfect morning is ruined by thoughts of *him*.

Caleb Adler is the last man I want on my mind.

Picturing anything about him makes my heart twist.

I sigh, mentally noting that in seven years since I last spoke to him, there have been approximately zero days without incident. The longest streak I've gone without memories of him crossing my mind is a measly two weeks.

In my defense, it's really damn hard to avoid thinking about an ex full stop when he's my best friend's brother...*and* is one of the top hockey players in the NHL.

Both make him difficult to evade. I've gone out of my way to dodge seeing him whenever our paths might cross, like coordinating with his sister if he's visiting our hometown to eliminate any chance where we'd have to interact and quickly changing the subject if hockey comes up. Despite those efforts to protect my heart, he still never leaves my thoughts for long.

"Want help with these, hon?" Leta asks.

The question pulls me from my thoughts. I paste on a beaming smile and shake my head.

"I've got it."

"You're sure? You're going to ice all of these by yourself?" She eyes me skeptically.

"Yeah, don't worry about it."

"We could get it done in half the time if we do it together."

"I've got a system. These will be finished in no time."

"Okay. You're the boss." She watches me work a moment longer before heading to open the shop for the day.

The Mrs. Claus themed designs are one of the biggest orders I've scored since I began offering custom cookies. I should accept the help, but some part of me has always struggled with letting others lend a hand. Even when I'm the first to offer mine.

It's a bad habit I've never outgrown as the eldest of three siblings. Hell of a leg-up for raising myself into a business woman. Terrible for maintaining any work-life balance or giving up control. It's just faster if I do it all on my own rather than trust someone else to meet the impossible standards I set for myself.

I push aside my internal cynic that questions why I hired extra help at all if I wasn't going to use it and allow myself to get wrapped up in decorating.

CHAPTER 2
CALEB

CONTRACT TERMINATED.

The reality of my NHL career going up in smoke over the last few days still hasn't hit me, even as my flight from Seattle lands in New York.

It's surreal to be close to my hometown in Vermont after playing hockey out there for six of the seven years I've done so professionally. In the span of less than a week I went from scoring the winning goal for our game against Minnesota to getting kicked off the team. Mid-fucking-season.

The last time my career was on the line for underperforming, I thought I was screwed. My prospect rankings were good in college, but I made it as a third round pick to a team that gave me little time on the ice and didn't reach the playoffs my rookie season.

Seattle was my fresh start thanks to a trade. I worked my way from the reserve list to the regular roster.

Now it's gone. What's worse, I wasn't fired as a result of my player record.

My phone feels like a ticking time bomb in my hand. For the time being, it's safe because it's off. As soon as that changes, boom. Game over.

I shift uncomfortably in the cramped economy seat and pull my cap down for the millionth time, worried people will recognize me.

The last thing I need is more speculation online about my swift dismissal from my team. The media already influences trades and signing deals as it is. The paparazzi running with the story has only poured gasoline on this PR storm.

It's made me a player no other team wants to touch. I swallow a bitter scoff. From one of the top prospect picks at twenty out of Heston U to the guy probably being sent down at twenty-seven because I didn't clear waivers for another team to take me. My jaw aches from how hard I've clenched it every time I replay what went down after the game.

The guy in the middle seat across from me keeps looking my way for longer than necessary. I avoid eye contact. I can't decide if it's a hey-isn't-that-Caleb-Adler stare or if he's willing the plane to reach the gate while mentally fighting the crowded flight to get off first.

Standing six foot five amongst a group of hockey players? I fit right in. But being a tall athlete traveling incognito? Way harder than I care for.

I swear I hear someone take a picture in my vicinity, the audible snapshot setting my teeth on edge.

Shit. I should've flown First Class.

After the fallout of the club siding with the shiny new rookie over my good intentions, I didn't want to wait around to find a more private seat. I booked the first open one I could find heading to the East Coast, not getting my hopes up for a one-way ticket home to Vermont. At least I lucked out with an aisle seat on a direct flight—it's a holiday miracle I didn't have a layover at another major hub.

The pinch of anxiousness has my strained muscles wound tight enough to cramp. Being cooped up on a plane for over five hours hasn't helped, only made everything worse.

I can't put it off forever. No matter how much I dread turning on my phone, I have to check in with my agent, Trevon, and let my family know in our group chat that my flight landed safely.

Just get it over with. Damn it. I power it on to let the world come flooding back in.

Out of habit, my thumb hovers over the text conversation I keep pinned to the top. The one I've never been able to bring myself to delete. It's remained there for years at this point. I open it when everything's getting to me and read her old texts.

Holly.

Being back on the East Coast means she'll be nearby. Will I see her? Hell, probably not. It's not like she'd want to see me. Seven years of silence from her has made that fact crystal clear.

I stare at the last thing she sent to me: Congratulations.

One clipped word, no emojis. So different from her usual radiant self. She sent it the day I was drafted to the NHL.

I thought all I ever wanted in life was to go pro playing hockey.

Once I got there, I never expected to realize too late how important other things were to me...like her.

Not until I lost her.

There have been so many moments I've wanted to talk to her. Wished I could see her again no matter how busy my life as a professional athlete is.

The only reason I've held back is the fear of seeing her beautiful features twisted in displeasure at a surprise visit from me. Any time I've been home during a break, it's noticeable that she avoids me. I've come to terms with the fact she wasn't in love with me and didn't think what we briefly had in secret was serious enough to hold on to, or she wouldn't have shut me out.

I need her more than she ever needed me, as much that truth crushes me.

I hate to admit that sometimes an irrational part of me is jealous of my sister, Layla, for getting to talk to Holly anytime she wants as her best friend.

Sometimes I tell her about my day only to delete the drafted message before sending. The things I don't have the balls to say in case I accidentally send the text is stored in my note app instead. One line for every time I've needed to say it. *I miss you.* Over and over again, countless entries over the years mixed with all the things I wish I could tell her.

I rub at the dull ache of regret in my chest and push aside the sense of something missing that always arises when she's on my mind.

When my phone connects to the network, it buzzes nonstop for a few seconds with a bombardment of messages from my teammates. Ex-teammates, I remind myself with an exhausted sigh.

Maybe I should've recognized how strongly I subconsciously had one foot out the door from the minute I got to Seattle.

Instead of putting down roots, I kept a sparsely furnished short-term lease rather than buy my own place, like most players once they make it to the big leagues. I put all my focus into the game, yet detached myself. The only thing I enjoyed out there was the hiking.

It's not like I made deep connections with most of the guys I played with, either. Not like I did with my Heston U boys when I was in college, because I still keep in touch with them. Other than Davy, my linemate and the guy I'm closest to, the rest were little more than co-workers.

Skimming through the texts wanting to know what happened, I pick Davy's. He was the one to hold me back the night it all went down with the rookie when I caught him getting pushy with a girl at the bar.

DAVY

What the fuck, bro? I just woke up to this.

He sends a link to the story announcing my contract termination with Seattle. The headline cites conduct issues between me and the newly acquired star rookie as the reason the team let me go. I scrub my face and tap out a reply.

CALEB

Sorry for not telling you. It all happened fast. When I took it to management, that little shit Chet had already gotten there ahead of me. They didn't believe my side of things. I guess since the rookie's family owns one of the club's biggest sponsors, they'd rather drop me instead of losing the money for that deal and Chet at the same time.

DAVY

Goddamn. Club politics are bullshit.

CALEB

Don't I fuckin' know it.

DAVY

I'm making Chet eat the ice at practice tonight. Where are you right now? Let's go grab a bite to eat.

CALEB

Thanks, but it'll have to be the next time I see you. My flight just landed in New York.

DAVY

Oh shit. You left?

CALEB

No point in staying there when I didn't clear waivers. If no other team is biting on me to buy out my contract, my agent wants me close by while he works his connections. Otherwise, I'll most likely be sent down.

. . .

The other teams must view me as a liability, despite all the work I've put into my career. If I'm lucky, Trevon will negotiate a new offer that keeps me playing at the NHL level.

Davy replies again, but I swipe out of the conversation before reading it. I'm not in the mood for platitudes when it's not like it's a skill issue that's burning my career to the ground. I made it through my rookie years and a trade. Then I solidified my place on this team with dedication, and my focus one hundred percent on honing my game.

This is where it gets me. Fired like I'm the bad guy, not Chet.

Swiping a hand over my mouth in agitation, I shuffle off the plane with the flow of passengers and keep my head bowed until I reach baggage claim.

As pissed off as I am about this mess...I don't regret my actions that landed me here. I'd do the same thing again in a heartbeat, because it made my blood boil to see the cocky rookie harassing the girl he was trying to take home. She wasn't interested in Chet, but he wasn't taking no for an answer. When I intervened and offered to escort her home safely, Chet started a fight with me that he couldn't finish.

He's the one with the fucking conduct issues. Not me.

I keep myself distracted by checking in with my family's group chat, scrolling back through the messages I've missed since I turned my phone off last night.

> **DAD**
>
> Mom made your favorite, kiddos. Except none of you are here, so I get it all to myself now hahaha.

> **LAYLA**
>
> Jokes on you, Dad. I know the recipe by heart and make it for dinner once a week.

> **DAD**
>
> [GIF of Homer Simpson compilation yelling Doh!]

> **ELIJAH**
>
> Seriously, who taught him where the GIF keyboard is? I just wanna talk...

> **LYLA**
>
> Yeah, that was me. No regrets. [Laughing emoji]

> **ELIJAH**
>
> Anyway, is that your way of saying you miss us? I sent you guys tickets and bought you flights for my game in Tampa so you both could have a nice weekend.

> **MOM**
>
> Ignore your father, sweetheart. I told him not to tease you kids. And thank you for the trip, Eli. It was a great time. You know we love getting to watch you and your brother playing. We're so proud.

> **LAYLA**
>
> What about me? Aren't you proud of me? No love for the middle child? [Sobbing emoji]

> **ELIJAH**
>
> Wait, who are you?

> **LAYLA**
>
> Shut up.

> **DAD**
>
> Of course we are, sweetie!!!!!!! You are the light of my life!!!! I'm so proud to be your dad!!!!

> **LAYLA**
>
> Mom, take his phone away. No one needs to use that many exclamation points.

My lips twitch reading through their conversation. The tangled knot in my chest loosens slightly. With a wry shake of my head, I tap out a quick message to let them know I've landed and will see them for Christmas in a couple of weeks. Hopefully the media storm will have blown over by then. Once I get out of here, I'm heading straight for our cabin in the Vermont mountains to ride it out.

People online can put whatever bullshit spin on things they want. It doesn't matter. I know I'll come out of this on the other side. Whatever it takes, I'll get back to the ice. To the game I love.

My stuff makes the slow parade around the baggage carousel, a small suitcase and an oversized equipment duffel. I cared more about making sure my gear was with me than packing clothes. I paid a service to ship whatever I left behind to a storage place in Candlewood, Vermont not far from my parents' place.

I wait it out until they're close, tracking the agonizingly slow crawl of the belt. At last, I grab my things and head for the car rentals.

Trevon calls while I'm waiting in line. I keep my voice low when I answer.

"Hey. What's going on?"

He snorts. "Not much, man. Just this player on my client list making me work for my dinner."

His wide, shining smile is easy to picture. It always lifts his cheekbones higher to crinkle the corners of his warm brown eyes.

I squeeze the back of my neck. "I said I was sorry."

"Didn't mean it, though, did you?" he fires back.

After a beat, I grunt. He chuckles.

"I'm just messing with you. Don't sweat it," he says.

"Easy for the guy who retired from the NHL with a stellar record to say," I reply.

His chuckle becomes a wheeze of amusement. "If I hadn't messed up my shoulder, I probably could've played another year or two, but then where would that leave you? Shit out of luck, that's where."

I've always appreciated this friendly vibe about him since he became my agent. He's like a big brother to me and it sets me at ease. I know he's got my back.

"I'm sure your husband is glad you spend your days in that cushy office instead of getting banged up at work," I say.

His smile is evident in his voice. "He's very appreciative, and the man loves to show it any chance he can."

The edge of my mouth lifts. "Is that why you let my calls go to voicemail midday sometimes?"

"Mind your business," Trevon answers smoothly. "Your flight landed twenty minutes ago. You know the drill: keep your head down while I deal with this."

I don't bother asking if he kept tabs on it. "I'm in line to pick up a rental, then I'm heading up to Mt. Helen where my family has a cabin."

It's a five hour drive from the city to northern Vermont on a good day. The weather report flashing on the airport monitors makes my stomach sink in resignation. It'll be five hours if I'm lucky, but I'm probably looking at spending the entire day on the road.

He makes an approving noise. "Good, good. Keep out of the public eye for the time being. I know you're itching to set the record straight, but hold it in for now. Give me a call when you get there. When I have something for you, I'll let you know."

"Got it." Exhaustion creeps into my tone.

"Like I said, don't sweat it. We're not done yet."

I nod even though he can't see it. "Thanks."

"And Caleb?"

"Yeah?"

"No gossip sites. Stay offline."

My jaw works. Too late for that. I've already stewed over some of the ridiculous articles.

"I heard that," Trevon admonishes.

"I didn't say anything."

"Exactly. I know you too well. Your silence said it all. I mean it, man. Stay the hell offline for your own good."

"Fine. I'm next in line. I'll talk to you later."

"Don't worry, kid."

"I'll try."

After hanging up, I blow out a breath and mute my notifications. The only thing standing between me and getting out of here is the rental agent at the counter who looks far too chipper this early in the morning.

CHAPTER 3
HOLLY

I'M in the zone through the early morning rush, restraining myself from poking my head out to check if Leta needs me several times. I do peek to see a few of the shop regulars enjoying their treats and grin to myself.

This is what made me fall in love with baking.

I taught myself how to do it by learning from online cooking videos. It was a way to entertain my younger siblings after school until our parents got home. The first time I watched my sister and brother's eyes light up as they enjoyed what I made, I was hooked. My passion has become a dream career for me at twenty-six.

It's not even 10 a.m. by the time I'm finishing the final dozen cookies in the order. Pride fills me, making me shake my generous ass with a bit more vigor while I victory dance before the last set.

With my height on the shorter than average side, my curvy hips tend to meet obstacles before the rest of me does. I'm so into grooving that I bump right into a rolling cart and nearly topple a tray of Mrs. Claus' tits. Thankfully, I save it before any fall.

"Close call," I say with a relieved chuckle. "Can't have my pretties going to waste."

"What are you doing back here?"

I jump at my brother's voice, endangering the rescued tray once more by almost knocking it over. "Shit!"

How long has Leo been standing in the back doorway? Definitely long enough to witness the near-miss with the cart.

Embarrassment heats my cheeks. The worst thing in the world is looking supremely uncool in front of your baby brother.

"Oh god. Pretend you didn't see any of that," I say.

"I didn't see that," he agrees. "But you may never live it down once I tell Hazel."

"Thanks," I reply sardonically.

Good thing our middle sister is usually on my side. Although, the two of them occasionally team up to tease me. If she does, I'll store the slight away for the perfect moment to dish out some sisterly payback. As siblings, we go to bat to protect one another from anything. But we're the only ones that are allowed to bust each other's chops. It's a unique form of family love.

"I'll just tell her you made it up since you don't have video proof. You scared the hell out of me," I chide.

"You were the one not paying attention to your surroundings."

He shrugs and swipes one of the glazed gingerbread muffins from a cooling rack. Those are supposed to replenish the counter once the first batch runs out. I give him a flat look that fades quickly once I see his dark blue eyes close with joy at the first bite.

He's not supposed to eat all my stock, but one muffin won't hurt. I'm betting he didn't eat breakfast before he left campus at the college he attends nearby. Knowing him, he rolled out of bed with just enough time to spare for a shower.

One of the reasons I gave him a job was to keep an eye on him to make sure he stays out of trouble, after all. He might be twenty now, but as his oldest sister I'm always going to feel like he's a little kid. It's up to me to take care of him.

It's just the two of us in Mayfield. Our parents live in our small hometown in Vermont a few hours away, and our sister is the only one they have near them in Candlewood. I should call Hazel to check in on how they're doing. I haven't talked to Mom in a couple of days.

Guilt pangs briefly in my chest. It's the same invisible weight I always suffer for moving here permanently instead of returning home after earning my degree.

Mayfield was supposed to be a temporary home while I went to college here, but I ended up loving it so much I didn't want to leave. Landing the perfect opportunity to open my bakery sealed the deal.

"You made it in on time today. Good job." I ruffle Leo's reddish-blond hair, smirking when he knocks my hand away with a grumble. Sibling balance restored. "Go sit down and finish your muffin. Do you want something to drink?"

"I'm good." He parks on a stool and scrolls on his phone while I put the finishing touches on the cookie order.

When I'm done, I finally take a seat for the first time since I came down to the bakery before dawn from my apartment above the shop. I could melt right on the spot from how quickly all my energy seeps from me. I didn't realize how exhausted I was until I slowed down.

Wincing, I roll my neck and rub the stiffness in my lower back from leaning over for so long. If I had any spare time for a spa day, I would love some pampering for once.

I jump to my feet when Leo starts bagging the Mrs. Claus cookies. "Don't forget to tie the bows. I put the ribbon over by the—"

"Okay, okay, okay. I get it. You've told me a hundred times, so you don't have to overexplain it again," he says.

"Sorry." I frown. "Thanks for doing that."

He nods. I prep a stack of sheer blush pastry bags and grab the spool of ribbon for him anyway to make his task easier.

As I'm checking the batches to see which ones are ready to be packaged, my phone buzzes with a call in my apron pocket. A photo of my best friend tossing confetti at the bakery launch fills the screen, drawing a smile from me.

"Those two tables are ready. These ones need more time to set," I tell Leo.

I wait for his acknowledgement before leaving through the back door. On my way out to the alley, I answer the call.

"Hi, sorry. I'm at work. What's up?"

"Oh, I know," Layla says in a matter-of-fact tone. "You at work is completely normal. It would be more shocking if you *weren't* working."

I hum, playing with the bow in my hair and bracing for another rehash of her trying to get me to take more than five minutes to rest. She's been texting me every day to see what my schedule would be this weekend.

"I don't mind being so busy," I say. "The extra business is great. Winter makes people want all the sweet, tasty treats. I like knowing things I've baked are being shared at all the holiday parties and special moments of the season."

She clicks her tongue. "That's exactly why I'm calling. When was the last time you took a vacation?" I start to answer, but she cuts me off. "Ah, ah! Janelle's bachelorette doesn't count. You were the one who planned the entire thing, and you barely took the time to enjoy yourself during the whole trip. And that was two years ago."

"Okay. You win." I bite my lip. "I don't remember the last time I actually took a vacation."

She pauses. "Who are you and what have you done with my workaholic best friend? You never admit it."

A chuckle huffs out of me. "So you're giving up?"

"Hardly. That makes it way easier to convince you to take some time off. Let's do a girls' weekend. We'll go to the cabin. It'll be so much fun." She grows more animated by the second.

The Adler's cabin holds so many good memories of trips I've taken with Layla and her family. Nostalgia wraps around me like a warm hug. The fresh Vermont mountain air is so peaceful and relaxing. Winter is my favorite time to be there when everything is gorgeous and magical, cloaked in snow. I've loved spending time there when her family has invited mine to join them to spend New Year's.

It's on the tip of my tongue to deny I need a break. Glancing through the window in the door at my brother packing efficiently, I wonder why I'm always so quick to do everything on my own.

"Come on, Hols. You need it," Layla says gently.

"Hell, you deserve it more than anyone. You're always taking care of everything. Let me do something nice for you for once. The bakery will be fine if you take a long weekend."

"I am ahead on my custom orders. But I don't know..."

One of the stray cats Marjorie feeds meows as she trots to me. She rubs against my leg and I crouch to pet her. She trills happily, purring as she rubs her cheek against my palm for more attention.

The to-do list constantly living in my head runs through the things that need my attention. I close my eyes with a sigh, but it's still there. It always is.

"I'm worried about you burning out. You've been saying you're so tired lately."

"I hear you," I murmur, entranced by how therapeutic petting the cat's soft fur is.

"So say yes," Layla urges. "It's been forever since we hung out, and we promised ourselves we wouldn't turn into the type of friends who never have time to see each other."

I only consider it for a beat longer before giving in. I do want to see her after spending the last year so focused on running the bakery I adore more than anything.

Leaving someone else in charge of the business I'm so proud of is nerve-racking, but I've earned a short break. If it's only for the weekend, Leo can handle things.

"You're right. Let's do it. Girls' weekend."

"You're in?" she gushes.

"I'm in."

Layla's squeal of excitement makes me laugh. It's infectious, making me bounce with my own eagerness.

A weight I wasn't aware of lifts from my shoulders at the idea of a charming cabin getaway.

CHAPTER 4
HOLLY

THE DRIVE to the cabin after lunchtime is breathtaking. I can't help drawing it out to enjoy the many scenic spots I pass on the way.

Some parts of the narrow switchbacks and steep icy roads are sketchy, though. Despite the white-knuckling moments navigating the last section of the trip taking me an extra twenty minutes, I make it there in time to admire the stunning afternoon sunlight hitting the recent snowfall blanketing everything.

This is so worth it. I'm feeling much less apprehensive about leaving Leo with a detailed guide to cover the weekend shifts.

With an excited squeal, I hop out of the car and take about a million photos of the glittering winter beauty. My

UGGs crunch through the fluffy snow as I explore the area around the driveway.

The view is incredible. I marvel at the sloping mountain range behind the cabin and the valley below from the rear of the wraparound porch. It's as if I'm in a giant snow globe, encased in magical serenity. Layla hasn't arrived yet, but she let me know the code for the key inside the lockbox and instructions for setting everything up.

It's even better inside the cabin. I pause on the threshold and take it in with a content sigh. The charming rustic accents are so comforting. My fingertips brush over the old leather armchairs by the cast iron wood burning fireplace. I can't wait to snuggle up by the fire with the book I brought.

This is going to be the best weekend. I'm so glad I finally listened to Layla. I really needed this.

I'm as enamored by the cozy atmosphere as I was when the Adlers invited me here in the past. Reminders of those summer and winter trips to the cabin with their family come rushing back.

I bite my lip around a smile when I think of the number of friendship bracelets I made with Layla with our feet dangling through the railing of the loft, swinging from a tire on a rope and swimming in the nearby lake with her brothers, chasing each other all through the surrounding woods. A laugh escapes me when I recall how much I hated getting poison ivy during one trip when we were young.

Although, the only person who spent the rest of that trip by my side to make sure I didn't scratch myself and helped me put on the ointment wasn't my best friend...it was her older brother.

I pick up a framed photo of Caleb from a mantel hung above the wood stove, tracing his charismatic smile with my thumb. The sharp cut of his jaw has always been a contrast to his easygoing nature. Thick brown hair flops across his forehead and his green eyes strike a pang in my heart.

If I close my eyes, I can still easily picture his rich laughter. My teeth catch my lip as the memory shifts to sneaking out in his truck and the feeling of that laughter warm against my throat before he trailed kisses along my skin.

I had always nursed a hopeless crush on him. Until one summer of flirting led to us crashing together passionately in secret, sneaking around late at night without telling anyone, swept up in the thrill of not getting caught together by Layla. Every fiery, perfect stolen moment lives vividly in my mind to this day.

He's not supposed to mean anything to me now.

It was an off-limits fling when we were young and impulsive, nothing more...no matter how much it stings to remind myself whenever I recall how much I liked his touch.

The frame clatters when I put it back on the shelf. My cheeks flush and I hurry back out into the chilly mountain air like my ass is on fire.

While I wait for Layla, I haul my bags inside along with the groceries I picked up. It begins to snow, light flurries at first that quickly turn to thick clumps that stick to my hair and clothes before I'm done. My UGGs will need to dry by the fire after getting so wet.

I'm slightly out of breath by the time I get the third one in. It's full of baking supplies because I thought I might bake for myself for once—something I haven't done in ages.

Perching on top of the suitcase, I survey what I brought. I might've overpacked out of eagerness for my first true vacation in—god, I'm not even sure how long.

"First things first..." Before I get too comfortable, I rise and prop my hands on my hips.

Where did Layla say the water main was again? I read through the steps she sent from her dad to open the cabin for use, and circle the outside twice before I find the part I'm supposed to turn on to connect the water supply line. With the steady snowfall, it's easy to miss. Mr. Adler's process sounds easy enough to handle on my own. I'll have this place ready to go in no time.

Just to be sure I know what I'm doing, I decide to search online for a video to walk me through it.

As I open my web browser, an alert banner with hockey news pops up. I flick it away with an annoyed huff without reading it. I set it up for updates about Caleb because I've followed his career. Maybe it's silly of me. Unfortunately, some part of me has always been unable to ignore him. I'm not in the mood to think about him for once.

I find a video with great visuals and figure out what to do. The buzz of success warms me from the inside. Thank you for always being my teacher in everything, internet.

The wood stockpiled in an open shed at the side of the cabin has enough stored for the weekend. Layla mentioned her dad wants us to chop more if we have the time to keep the supply replenished.

I eye the axe hanging from a hook curiously. I've never tried it, but it could be fun. The idea of swinging a sharp object around and splitting wood might be therapeutic. Throw in a little screaming and it sounds like a party. Until the nearest neighbor thinks I'm being murdered by a wild animal.

Grinning to myself, I grab an armful of wood and I head back inside to start a fire and warm up. The dampness in my soft woolen boots is seeping through to my socks, and I need to get them off before I have a sensory meltdown.

Several attempts later, I'm struggling and getting nowhere.

I thought starting the wood stove would be the easy part. I'm a baker, I deal with heat all the time. Yet all the kindling I try snuffs out before the logs catch fire. The best I manage is making them smoke.

"Okay, why can't I get this?" I fold my arms and frown at the ancient cast iron fireplace, parking my butt on the floor to think.

It always seemed easy when Layla's parents or brothers got a fire going. So what am I doing wrong?

When in doubt, to the web. I won't fail.

I'm going to conquer this and stoke a fire so cozy I doze off reading because I'll be too damn comfy.

Pursing my lips, I give a sharp nod of determination. I'm resourceful. There's nothing I can't figure out on my own when I put my mind to it.

My brows knit in confusion when my search takes forever. I realize why once I see the error symbol in the top corner of my phone screen. The cell service is much spottier than it was when I arrived. I can't get the internet to load at all.

"Oh, really?" I groan. "Why now?"

I scramble to my feet to see if I can find a signal, only to slump face first over the arm of the couch in defeat. It's time to regroup and make a yummy snack so I can think better. At least using the oven will provide some warmth in the chilled cabin.

I change out of my jeans and pull on some extra layers, shrugging into a chunky knit cardigan with fuzzy pastel baubles. While I'm unpacking my baking supplies on the kitchen counter, I peer out the window.

It's snowing even harder than it was before, and visibility is dwindling with the fading light. I grab my phone and call Layla to check in with her when I have bars in that spot.

"Hey," she answers on the second ring, sounding frazzled. "I've been trying to call you. Did you make it to the cabin?"

"Yeah, I got in a little over an hour ago," I say.

"Oh good." She sighs with relief. "I was worried about you on those tight roads."

"They're a bitch to maneuver, but I did it. It's snowing here. Cell service is getting spotty. I guess it's because it's really coming down out there now."

"I know. It's snowing everywhere," she replies. "There's a huge storm system moving in that's colliding with the nor'easter coming up the coastline. The news is calling it the blizzard of the decade."

I pause my organization of mulling spices. "Didn't they call the back to back super snowstorms last year the blizzard of the decade?"

"This one's going to set even bigger snowfall records," she says.

I glance out the window, trying to make out the view I admired earlier. I can barely see past the hot tub on the porch to the stone fire pit in the yard. My thoughts stray to the intense weather all over that continues to set unprecedented records as our planet warms. Extreme snowstorms, devastating flooding, unbelievably powerful hurricanes, and the threat of tornadoes all wreaking havoc.

"So where are you right now? Did you have to stop at a hotel for the night?" I ask.

"Worse, I never made it out of town," she answers miserably. "I'm sorry. Dad called me and told me not to drive anywhere."

"You're not on the road, so that makes me feel better."

Disappointment lingers. It's not her fault, but the unexpected change in plans rouses my anxiety. Looks like I'll be spending the weekend by myself.

"What about you? This is so not how I wanted our girls' weekend to go. I feel awful."

"I know. But maybe if the storm passes quickly, you'll still make it up here," I suggest hopefully.

"I'll be there in a heartbeat. You'd better send me regular updates. Promise me you'll stay put and relax, okay?" Layla prompts.

"I'm bummed you aren't here, but I'll still make the best of my solo retreat," I swear with a smile. "In fact, I'm already on it. I'm going to make mulled wine and I brought books to read."

"Oh, I almost forgot to tell you. You won't be totally alone."

My grin falls. "What? Why?"

"Because—"

The line dips in and out, garbling her voice. Then the call drops. I frown at my phone and set it aside with a sigh. Maybe she meant that the neighbor who owns the farm nearby will be around if I want some company.

Before I decide what to whip up, a rustling sounds at the side of the cabin. I freeze, listening carefully. It moves onto the porch.

"A bear?" I whisper in disbelief. "What the fuck? Shouldn't they be hibernating?"

It can't get in, right?

Something heavy scrapes the floorboards on the porch. Shit. I wish I still had Layla on the phone, at the very least for some moral support.

I grab the closest thing I have—a rolling pin and the bowl to my standing mixer—to make enough noise to scare it off.

"Okay, it's chill. You're fine. You can do this."

Taking a breath to strengthen my courage, I peek through the door. With the heavy snowfall and how dark it is now, it's hard to make out the bulky shape edging closer. It's halfway to the door.

Oh, hell. It's now or never.

Opening the door a crack, I shriek as loud as I can and clang the rolling pin against the metal bowl.

The shape startles with a very human bellow.

He almost loses his footing, clutching a duffel bag strap. It's not a bear attack after all.

The relief is short lived when I realize if it's not a wild animal, I'm dealing with a man alone in the mountains with no one else around for miles.

Is he a burglar? A murder? An escaped convict? I don't even know if there's a prison around here, but my freaked out mind splinters in countless directions, running through the potential ways men are dangerous in wooded settings.

This creep isn't getting me.

Adrenaline surges through me. Steeling my frazzled nerves, I do the only thing I can think of, acting before he has the chance to do anything to me first.

Heart pounding, I bolt forward and take a swing at him with my rolling pin.

The intruder chokes back a surprised noise at my attack, muttering a confused curse. His reflexes are sharp enough to catch my wrist to stop me from whacking him over the head. He's much stronger than me, causing me to freak out even more.

"No!" I struggle, making a fist to jab him.

"Just—I'm not—Stop," he grumbles in exasperation

while wrangling me before I get a hit in. Best I manage is elbowing his gut, earning a satisfying grunt. "I'm not here to hurt you."

Wait—I recognize that voice.

My scrappy retaliation ceases, chest heaving raggedly as I drag my apprehensive gaze to meet familiar green eyes, a handsome chiseled jaw, and unruly thick brown hair I used to love running my fingers through.

"No. No fucking way." The raw whisper slips out of me before I check my inside thoughts.

My heartbeat quickens again, racing so fast I fear I might pass out from shock. He's no burglar...he's Layla's brother.

The star hockey player in the NHL I grew up with. The one man I never wanted to see again after he broke my heart.

"Caleb?" I yelp. "What the hell are you doing here?"

CHAPTER 5
CALEB

AFTER THE WEEK I've had, I honestly didn't expect to end it almost taking a hit from a rolling pin of all things. The drive from the airport took all day. I'm bone fucking tired after traffic, loading up on groceries, and getting recognized at the store.

I expected to be alone here.

But I can't help the grin that breaks free at the sight of Holly Duncan huffing and puffing in front of me. The porch light catches her blue eyes glittering with indignation. Strands of pink hair fall loose from her ponytail tied up with a bow. The urge to tuck them behind her ear is strong.

She took a swing at me, but somehow I feel like laughing.

"Holly."

Her name falls from my lips tinged with too many emotions to pick apart. Surprise. Delight. Relief.

Longing I've kept buried from everyone.

For the first time in days, the apprehensive weight bearing down on me eases.

"Are you kidding me? That's all you have to say for yourself?" She smacks my chest with the hand I'm not holding hostage. "Not 'hey, sorry for not announcing myself and *scaring the absolute shit out of you*. You know, like I should—because I'm America's considerate, favorite fucking hockey sweetheart. I'm waiting."

A bolt of all too familiar desire sparks low in my abdomen at her spitfire nature.

She's still as mouthy as ever.

And it seems I'm still as into it as ever.

I'm thrown back to the first time that perfect little mouth finally made me lose control, forgetting all the reasons she was off-limits as my sister's best friend because I had to kiss her.

Time apart from her hasn't altered a thing. The need to kiss her now is alive and fucking well, reigniting in my chest like it has a proximity alert to the girl I've secretly missed every day since I fumbled her. Idiot move on my part.

"You haven't changed." I take my time admiring her, drinking her in like a starved man finding my salvation.

She bristles. I cough to cover a chuckle and suppress

how much it makes me want to get under her skin more. I've always liked riling her up to test her limits.

There's zero chance I get it together. Five seconds in her presence and I'm already gone. Maybe that makes me a pathetic guy still pining after my ex-girlfriend for years after I let her slip through my fingers, but I don't care. Not when she's right in front of me at last.

"I would've told you it was me, but you didn't give me a chance. You took one look and went all battle cry on me before I could get a word in," I point out.

"I thought you were a bear!"

I tilt my head with a smirk. "As you can see, not a bear."

"And then when I realized you weren't, I thought you were a burglar or creep coming to attack me." She slumps after snapping, exhaling heavily. "I think you took about five years off my life, minimum. What are you doing here?"

"Going to my cabin. You know, because it's my family's place," I offer in a deadpan tone.

"No, I mean *here*—like, back in New England."

Has she not seen the news? Maybe she doesn't follow hockey stuff. The thought brings as much relief as it does a hollow feeling carving out the space behind my ribcage. On one hand, it means she won't know why I'm holing up here to avoid the PR storm. On the other, there's the possibility she hasn't seen even one of my professional games.

"Are you still planning on hitting me with the rolling pin?" I murmur.

My thumb traces the inside of her wrist. Her lashes flutter and she sways into me. I picture myself tilting her chin up and sealing my mouth over hers in a kiss.

The fantasy vanishes a moment later as she regains her composure and leans back to put as much space between us as she can while I've got her wrist in my grip. She opens and closes her mouth a few times, then huffs.

"I haven't decided yet. But if I do, I'm warning you now that you absolutely deserve it." She narrows her eyes and lifts her chin.

"I bet."

At my gravelly chuckle, a new fuse sparks to life in those beautiful eyes. Pursing her lips, she jostles her hand. I hold on, grinning when she tugs harder without getting anywhere. Just to mess with her, I tuck it against my chest.

"Caleb," she grumbles.

"Holly," I reply smoothly in amusement.

"Damn it," she grits out. "Let go of me."

"Whatever you want, sugar cookie."

I miss the shape of her wrist the instant my fingers loosen to release her hand. She wrenches it away, then shuffles a few pointed steps back on the porch while brandishing the rolling pin. I want to reach out and touch her again, like I have so many times when she entered my dreams over the years.

"What's wrong? Worried I bite?" My tongue traces my lower lip. "You know I only do that when you ask for it nicely."

Holly groans, crossing her arms. "I see you haven't changed one bit, either. Still a cocky ass who thinks you can flirt your way out of anything."

I rub my jaw. "Yeah? You used to like it last I checked."

"Not anymore." The blaze in her eyes burns bright and hot. "Never again."

The words hit me square in the chest harder than any check during a game.

She's the one that walked away from us.

But I'm the one who let her go without chasing after her harder when she stopped responding to my messages because I thought hockey was the only thing I wanted in life.

I rub at the sharp sensation scraping the inside of my sternum and clear my throat. "So, are you going to let me in?"

"I should make you sleep in your car," Holly mumbles testily.

"If that's what you want me to do, I will."

It'll be cold as fuck, but I'll manage. If she needs time and space to cool down, I can do that for her.

Her lips part and her gaze softens from anger to surprise. She eyes me like she's waiting for me to take back the offer, because no one in their right mind sleeps outside during a blizzard when there's shelter right there.

She whirls around and heads for the door. "Let's go in. It's too cold out here, and I don't want my clothes getting wet with snow again."

I follow her inside, setting my equipment bag and suitcase next to the shoe rack my grandpa carved when I was a kid. My family's cabin smells exactly the same as I remember, like being wrapped up in nature by the scent of cedar mixed with pine and woodsmoke. It's comforting to be back after so much time away. I spent countless summers here. It's one of my favorite places.

As I survey every familiar corner, I pause on the cast iron fireplace. There are logs inside, but no fire crackling.

Toeing off my boots so I don't track snow across the hardwood floor—my grandmother and mom's admonishments a permanent echo in my head—I take a knee and open the door. The logs are stacked in a way that traps airflow and there are ashen remains of several fire starter scraps.

"How long have you been here?" I ask.

Holly leans over the island separating the kitchen from the sitting area. "I got to enjoy the peace of having the cabin all to myself for one whole hour before you showed up."

The corner of my mouth lifts. She goes back to organizing baking supplies and ingredients on the counter. I'm momentarily distracted by the sweater she has on, fingers twitching with the urge to play with the dangling bow strings at the neckline. I register how many layers she's wearing and connect the dots with the lack of burning wood to heat the place.

"Did you have trouble starting the fire?"

Something clatters in the kitchen and she blurts several curses under her breath. I cover my mouth and try to smother the smile on the verge of breaking free.

As I rearrange the logs, I explain, "There are different ways to stack your firewood. It helps it catch easier and ensures it burns efficiently. You did a good job. You almost had it."

She mutters something from behind me after creeping closer to watch. It sounds like she's parroting my instructions in a mocking tone to herself.

I move so she can see what I'm doing better and point out the optimal method for starting the fire. She crouches beside me, taking in the information despite the fact she doesn't look happy about me being the one to teach her.

My entire side heats with awareness of her close proximity. It would take nothing to close the small gap just to feel her shoulder bumping into my arm.

"See? You just needed to make an adjustment to put the bigger pieces at the bottom, and orienting them this way in the stove will keep it burning all night long."

Her eyes narrow. "I would've figured it out eventually."

"I know. You've always been a smart girl."

She catches me watching her and looks away before I can hold her gaze longer. I light the kindling and keep an eye on the logs until they catch. When I'm satisfied with the growing flames, I ease the door shut and peer at her from my periphery.

Holly closes her eyes in contentment, shuffling closer to the fireplace.

"Better?" I ask softly.

Her mouth tugs down at the corners and she reaches across me to pull her damp boots closer to the stove. "I could've done this without you. I just got sidetracked."

I smirk. The attitude she gives me isn't off-putting in the slightest. Her sharp tongue has always captivated my desire. It feels like warm maple syrup spilling into my stomach. I push my fingers into my hair to keep from tracing the shape of her mouth to relearn it.

"Do you want any help with that stuff in the kitchen? Looks like you were about to make something."

"I'm going to stay here for a minute." She begins shedding her extra sweater layers. "This feels so nice."

Her hum fills my head with dirty ideas of all the ways I can get her to make that sound again, each one more appealing. Hell, I need a distraction before a simple noise from her gives me a boner.

Entertaining fantasies of her for years is going to make my self control go to shit finally having the real deal in front of me again.

I busy myself taking my stuff to one of the bedrooms upstairs, leaving the biggest one for her. There are a few missed messages hidden within my muted notifications that came in hours ago. The internet's out and there's no cell signal when I check my phone, which is fine by me. I want to be shut off from the world.

Trevon sent me a text around when I stopped for gas, before it started snowing hard. He says the snowstorm will delay the meetings he's working on by a few days. I also have a couple of missed texts from my sister a few hours apart.

LAYLA

I heard you're going to stay at the cabin. Me and Holly have a girls' weekend planned, so I'm warning you now to be chill. And we get dibs on the hot tub.

LAYLA

Weekend plans update...I won't be making it. But Holly left way earlier than me. Last time she checked in with me, she was almost there. Be nice to my bestie!

My head jolts with a snort. Yeah, be nice to her.

No problem. I'll play nice. Always have.

Layla never caught me sneaking around with Holly the summer she was mine. We didn't last long enough to ever tell her. As far as she's concerned, she's the only connection between us. She's never noticed that any time she's mentioned Holly, I hang on every word, tucking away every scrap of information she shares in passing.

I sprawl on the bed and listen for sounds of my sister's best friend downstairs. It'll be just the two of us for however long the snowstorm keeps us here.

There's only one issue: I want to be *so nice* to Holly that she lets me untie all her little bows and remind her I know exactly how to make her unravel.

CHAPTER 6
HOLLY

IN THE MORNING, I have to face the reality of the situation. I stand at the window of the bigger bedroom—thank you, Caleb, for being a gentleman—taking in the heaps of snowfall the blizzard dumped on us overnight. And it's still going without any sign of letting up.

We're snowed in.

There's no denying it when I can't even see the stone fire pit on the sloping hill behind the cabin anymore.

And we're going to be stuck here for longer than my planned weekend. *Together.*

I don't think Caleb is awake yet. It's pretty early. I've been up for an hour watching the sky get lighter after pulling Mrs. Adler's favorite sitting chair over to the window, snuggling under the blanket draped over it. I've always been a morning person and I'm used to my schedule for the bakery.

This time of day is usually my serene bubble.

I wind the blanket tassels around my fingers as I stare at the weather I'm powerless to change. I hate sitting still when I want to take action somehow. The lack of control is tying my stomach in knots.

I wanted a break. What do I get? Trapped with my best friend's brother. Actually, worse, since he's my ex.

Worries keep plaguing me about what this means for the bakery. I'm not sure when it can open unless I trust my brother and Leta to continue running things without me. A new cinch pulls tight in my stomach.

Biting my lip, I check my phone again. At least the power hasn't gone out. Caleb mentioned last night before we went to bed that the cabin has a back up generator with plenty of solar charge to keep the cabin running for days if we lose power.

Still no cell signal.

Sighing, I draft a message to Leo and Leta explaining that my weekend might be extended because I'm stranded in the mountains. Plus a rundown of everything I do to open and close the bakery for the day. Both are ready to send it the moment I connect to enough bars.

Thank god I brought some supplies with me. I was caught up on orders before impulsively taking the trip, but if we're here more than a few days I'll need to make sure I don't fall behind.

It's close to 8 a.m. and I still haven't heard a peep of movement from Caleb's room next door. If I strain my ears, I can make out the soft reverberation of his snores. Pulling a face, I climb out of my blanket cocoon. I need coffee before I drive myself up the wall, and if he's not waking up I'm not making any for him.

I slip my feet into the fuzzy cream pair of slippers I packed, sparing a fleeting smile for the embroidered red bows. Braving the invisible boundary line of the bedroom door, I quietly step into the hall.

Pausing at Caleb's door, I sigh. I'm not a total bitch. I'm not going to deprive him of coffee after he showed me how to light the fire properly.

"Caleb?" I knock, softly at first, then a bit harder when there's no answer. Rolling my eyes, I try again and mutter, "Are you going to sleep the day away, heartbreaker?"

A thump sounds inside, followed by a groan of pain. My eyes widen when it seems as if he staggers to the door before wrenching it open.

Oh, wonderful. My best friend's brother is shirtless.

Bleary-eyed and sleep mussed, he's still the most hand-some man I've ever seen.

My heart skips a beat as my gaze trails from his tousled brown hair to his amazing jawline covered in stubble. I can't stop, following his bobbing Adam's apple to the expanse of his broad shoulders. I lose myself in admiring his bare chest and forget how to breathe for a second.

Damn it. Caleb is still frustratingly attractive and it's impossible to ignore. He's tormenting me with those gray sweatpants hanging low on his hips, impressive dickprint fully on display.

I do not want to climb him like a tree. I do not want to climb him like a tree. I absolutely *do not* want to climb Caleb fucking Adler like a sexy mountain man tree and find out if my eyes are deceiving me, or if that bulge in his slutty gray sweatpants is bigger than I remember.

"Hi," I stammer, hoping he doesn't notice I'm practically drooling over him.

Keep cool, Holly. Chill. Like a cheesecake. Or rum custard. Great, now I'm turned on *and* hungry.

"Wha'ssit?" He yawns, scratching his abdomen where dark hair leads down into the slouched waistband of his pants.

I blurt the first thing that springs to mind. "You're shirtless. I mean—It's morning."

"Morning," he repeats drowsily. "Stubbed my damn toe getting up. Forgot about the legs on the nightstand. Always gets me."

I nod in sympathy, too stunned by the sight of his chiseled physique to form a snappy response. "Bastard furniture."

He hums in agreement, casually bracing an arm overhead in the doorway. My mouth goes completely dry.

Oh my god. I'm screaming inside.

Was he always this hot?

Always so generously toned and—I can't believe I'm admitting this even in my head—so tempting?

He wasn't, right? He couldn't possibly have been this fit the last time I saw him when we were in college.

I'd pinch myself to see if I'm in one of the pesky dreams featuring him, but having his hooded green gaze focused intently on me is making it hard to think. He draws in a deep breath, releasing it with a pleased rumbling exhale before leaning in like he's going to kiss me.

"Caleb." I stop whatever he's trying to pull with a hand on his firm stomach.

He covers it with his palm, holding my touch against his skin. His body is so much warmer than my cold fingers, and he smells incredible. The rich, earthy aroma blended with pine makes my knees weak.

"Caleb." His name comes out a bit breathless this time.

He stills, clearing his throat as he releases his grasp. "Sorry. Takes me a minute to fully wake up. Can't get used to it, even after all the morning skates on my schedule."

I recall how his mom would send me, Layla, and our

friend Hana into his room on the weekends to make sure he didn't sleep all day. It took forever to pull him from slumber deeper than the dead.

"I remember." Ignoring how nice his muscles felt, I back down the hall. "I'm making coffee. Come down if you want some."

"Sounds good. I'm going to shower, then I'll join you."

Once his door closes, I haul ass to the first floor. I don't stop until I brace my hands on the sink, taking several breaths to calm my racing heart. If I hadn't stopped him, I'm certain he was going to kiss me.

A warm flutter stirs in my stomach.

I don't want to admit to myself whether or not I would've let him.

If I did, I'd only get hurt again. I have to stay strong.

Once a heartbreaker, always a heartbreaker. There's no second chances for us. Especially not for Christmas.

CHAPTER 7
HOLLY

"Coffee," I decide. "I need coffee to deal with all of this."

I do a stellar job not picturing Caleb's muscled body with water droplets rolling over every delectable inch of skin. He's always been irresistibly handsome, but he's only gotten better with age. His body is more muscled and his cute boyish features have become more defined.

I'm concentrating so hard on *not* thinking about it, that he startles me when he pokes my side from behind.

Shrieking, I spin around, finding him bundled in a Fair Isle sweater and jeans. He holds his hands up apologetically.

"Jesus Christ, Caleb. Are you actually on a mission to give me a heart attack?" I clutch my chest dramatically.

"I didn't realize you were lost in thought. I wasn't quiet coming down," he says sheepishly. "My bad."

"It's fine. Here." I hand him a mug. "It's still just cream, no sugar, right?"

The side of his mouth lifts and his eyes crinkle at the corners. A dreamy dimple appears in his cheek. I avert my attention, adding a cinnamon stick to my mug.

"You remembered how I take my coffee?"

"It's just coffee. Don't make a big deal out of it. I happen to have a good memory for random stuff, that's all. I'm sure you don't still have mine memorized."

"Of course I do."

My gaze snaps back to him. He grins.

"Your go to is a latte with oat milk and honey, or two pumps of whatever flavor syrup is your favorite of the moment. You also love the specialty seasonal stuff."

He nods to the cinnamon stick in my coffee and winks at my gaping expression.

"Show off," I mumble.

A memory flits across my mind of the times he'd text me to meet up in secret, always surprising me with a drink just because he knew I liked it or my favorite snacks stashed in his glove compartment. I bury it, forgetting how those small gestures used to make me swoon over him. He probably did it for all of his hookup partners.

Caleb takes his coffee to the front porch. I follow him out, tucking my oversized cardigan around me to keep the cold at bay. Snow drifts have formed up the steps. It reaches almost up to the wheels of our cars, and they're both SUVs.

"Nothing beats this, huh? I forgot how gorgeous it is up here at this time of year," he says.

He seems far less stressed by this storm than I am, taking in the scenic winter view appreciatively. It is beautiful when I set aside the worry running on hamster wheels in my brain.

"Don't you have hockey games? It's not winter break yet," I say.

His attention shoots to me. "That's true."

I roll my lips between my teeth, not wanting to admit I have an alert on my phone that tracks NHL news for mentions of him.

"So, what—they put in a substitute player for you?"

His jaw works and he stares into the woods. "I'm...on leave. There's already a player taking over my spot for games."

"Oh."

Curiosity bubbles within me. I want to ask what that means and why he's on a break from the sport he loves. His body language holds me back. The stiff set of his shoulders gives me the hint he doesn't want to talk about it right now.

Squinting at the sky, he gives a low whistle. "I'd say we're snowed in indefinitely if this doesn't let up by tomorrow."

"How long is indefinitely?" I ask through a new wave of anxiety.

"Last time I was up here for a storm like this, it was weeks before I could go anywhere."

"Like, more than two weeks? That means we'll be stuck here for Christmas." My grip on my mug tightens. "I don't know if my brother can run my bakery for that long. How am I going to get my customers' orders out?"

"Hey, take it easy." He rests a hand on my shoulder, squeezing supportively. "It might not be that long. It depends on when the blizzard passes and when the roads are cleared. Until then, we ride it out."

As much as I don't want his help, he has a point. It allows me to calm down a little.

Out of nowhere, the distressed honk of a goose interrupts the steady *tink* of frozen snowflakes hitting the ground.

"Was that a goose?" I look around, both curious and a bit worried there's an animal out in the storm. "I think it's coming from the wood shed."

"Hang on."

He sets his coffee down, then ducks inside for his coat and boots. Without a moment's hesitation, he wades off the porch into the thick snow. Even with his towering height, it's almost to his knees in some spots as he trudges over to the side of the cabin to investigate. I move to the corner of the porch to watch.

"Oh, Greta," Caleb croons woefully a few moments later. "Did you come to see me and got stuck?"

I can't see her, but the goose honks in response. He speaks soothingly to the bird he apparently knows by name, moving chopped wood until he has enough room to scoop a big white goose from the walled side protected from the storm.

"There we go," he says.

"Is she okay? Was she trapped in there overnight?"

"Maybe. There's a pond nearby she usually forages at. Doesn't seem like she's dehydrated." He holds her beneath his arm, examining her while she squawks with attitude. "She was probably out looking for food once it started snowing and got herself wedged once she was in there."

He carries her onto the porch and dusts snowflakes from her feathers, then uses his coat to bundle her. After several bouts of animated honking while he talks to her fondly, she settles, even letting him pet her.

I don't know what to do with myself while it all goes down.

"So, you're hugging a goose," I say.

Caleb chuckles. "This is Greta. She lives on the neighbor's farm at the next cabin up, about two miles away. Want to say hi?"

I like animals, but geese sort of intimidate me. I edge closer, waving awkwardly.

"Hi, Greta."

The goose turns her frighteningly perceptive blue eyes on me, giving a single, indignant honk. It feels judgmental. And like she's warning me to stay away from Caleb.

He laughs. "I won't let her bite you."

"She bites?" I take a step back and shake my head.

"No. Well..." He strokes her feathers. "Only once. I warned Layla not to hold her hand like that when she was feeding her."

"Sure, that makes me feel better. How do you know her?"

"This pretty girl's been in my life for years," he says.

I remind myself he's talking about the bird and not some other woman, extinguishing the hot rush of jealousy I have no right to feel.

"I was around nineteen when her mom was showing her how to free range when she was a gosling. She got tangled in some of my grandpa's fishing netting and was making such a racket until I found her. I think she liked the sound of my voice because she sat patiently in my lap while I worked the netting free."

All the times I came here with Layla and I had no idea her brother formed a close bond with this goose. He's so sweet with her. The touching scene makes me slide my lips together, fighting back the urge to swoon over a man who's good with animals. Curse my hormones for being hardwired to find everything about him attractive.

"I didn't realize geese lived so long," I say.

"Same. They're pretty amazing. The neighbor told me all about his flock when I brought her back to him. They forage for up to three miles away, so after I rescued her I guess she considered our property as part of her territory. She goes back to her roost at night, usually."

"Wow. That's impressive."

"Right? She's a smart girl."

"Why does she go off on her own if she has a flock?" I wonder.

"She's just independent according to Jim. I had the same question the first few times she was here. He told me sometimes flock birds feel better off on their own."

A pang squeezes my heart. My throat thickens with a tangle of understanding and melancholy. I didn't expect to relate to a goose, but here I am getting misty-eyed.

I swallow the lump clogging my throat. "So what do we do? Take her back?"

"I'll make a shelter for her in the storage shed so she's warm and dry, at least until the storm blows over. Once it does, I'll make the hike to get her home."

He gets to work, leaving me alone with Greta. I take a seat nearby on the porch swing, sipping my coffee. She nestles into his jacket, honking at me in warning again.

"Be cool, Greta. I don't want your man. He's all yours."

Greta quirks her head. A laugh huffs out of me.

It doesn't take long for Caleb to rearrange the shed tucked between the trees at the edge of the driveway. I kid myself pretending I'm not watching him shovel snow to make a path from the shed to the porch. Even wearing a sweater, his athletic build is clearly in peak condition. I'm entranced by the appealing flex of his shoulders and biceps paired with the hot grunts of effort as he completes the task.

Warmth simmers in my veins. Once he's done, he pulls out a hatchet to cut some pine branches which he seems to use for insulating the shelter he's creating for Greta.

The competence is undeniably alluring.

"Okay, Greta," he announces when he's finished. "Home sweet shed. You can head in, Holly. I'll be right behind you after I get the freeze-proof bowls from my dad's camping gear to give her water."

"You don't need any help?"

"I'm good."

My lips purse to one side and I hesitate at the door. "I have plenty of oats I brought to bake with. Can we give her that?"

He flashes me a crooked smile. "Yeah. Thanks."

Feeling useful, I hurry inside to prepare a meal for a goose. While I'm portioning some oats into a wide bowl, I peek in the fridge to see what else I can give her. There's some fresh spinach that, honestly, I was only bringing so we'd feel like there was some nutritional balance between the goodies I planned to whip up for girls' weekend. I also add a small handful of cranberries and find a bag of frozen peas in the freezer to thaw.

Caleb's handsome features light up when I bring the food out. "This is great, sugar."

My stomach dips and heat blooms in my cheeks. "It's nothing."

Hopefully he thinks I'm blushing because it's winter, not because of his praise.

Our hands brush when he takes the bowl. He lingers and rubs my fingers with his thumb. I jerk away, rushing into the haven of the cabin to put some much needed space between us.

Not long after, he comes in without a word about... whatever that momentary relapse in sanity was. I know I'm still in hell when he changes out of snow-covered jeans back into slutty gray sweatpants.

"Breakfast?" he suggests, entirely unaware I'm fighting for my life not to drool over him more than I have this morning.

"Breakfast. Yes," I agree, too cheery and forced for him not to notice.

I become a whirlwind of movement in the cozy

kitchen, pulling out pans and cooking utensils, grabbing at random from the groceries we both brought. If I keep active, I don't have to acknowledge the way his green eyes track me.

He catches me by the shoulders. My heart doesn't stop racing, picking up speed at the warmth of his body nearly touching my back.

"Sit. I'll make it," he murmurs.

"I can do it," I say automatically.

I'm used to making everyone food. It's a habit engrained in me to always assume if we're eating, I'm the one feeding people.

"I'm sure you can. But let me handle it today."

"Do you even know how? I thought you were too busy playing hockey."

His lips twitch with amusement. "I know what I'm doing. I've picked up a few other skills over the years."

To my shock and awe, he's not bluffing.

Caleb looks way too good with his sleeves pushed up and a moose print tea towel slung over his shoulder while managing two pans at once on the stove. This is unfair and unusual punishment first thing in the morning.

The delectable scent of bacon and eggs crackling away in the frying pan mixed with the sweet note of cinnamon pancake batter he's mixing is making my mouth water.

It's definitely the food, not how hot and laid-back he is multitasking. He surprised me with food in the past, but he's never cooked a meal for me before. This version of him is more mature than the one who kissed me when he was twenty. It's throwing me off-kilter.

I still want to offer my help, feeling like I should be doing something. He interrupts me before I make it to where my apron hangs.

"I've got this. You sit down and relax," he insists smoothly.

Letting someone else do things for me is strange, but I perch on a stool at the island to watch him cook. "How did you know I was hungry?"

"Because I pay attention," he answers as he flips a pancake.

I swallow and occupy myself by pinching the chunky knit baubles on my fuzzy cardigan so I don't have to think about what he sees if he's watching me closely...or how nice his muscles are when they flex with a spatula in hand. How will I survive being snowed in with him if the little things are testing my resolve?

"You've always been grouchy if you aren't fed since we were kids, and food is usually the answer to making most things better." He laughs to himself, the rich sound stirring a flutter in my stomach. "Not that I don't have a thing for that mouth of yours when you get going. Don't worry, I'll make sure you don't go hungry as long as you're with me."

My heart skips a beat when he pins me in place with a look. It's tinged with confidence and familiar desire, reminding me how well he learned everything about me, back when I believed we fit well together. Heated memories I've locked away from years ago replay in my head without my permission. Every blazing touch, every intense kiss permanently etched on a piece of me that can't forget about him.

This is a part of Caleb that has always been attractive to me. When I have his attention, it's all mine and no one else's. He gives his all to the person he's with, anticipating their needs. I forgot how much I liked it not having to be the one in charge of everything for once.

He holds my gaze for another beat. Then the corner of his mouth quirks up as his focus travels to my lips, lingering a moment before he returns to the food he's making.

Damn Caleb and his disarming charm. He knows he's getting under my skin. I saw that satisfied smirk.

Sure, he put me first for one whole summer when we were in college. It was exhilarating sneaking around with him.

But those few months seven years ago were all we had until I overheard him downplaying our short-lived relationship during a call with his coach. He went back to Heston University in the fall to keep playing hockey, and by the following summer he was drafted into the NHL.

Good for him. I didn't need him then and I don't now,

because without him I achieved my own dreams by opening my bakery.

We might be stuck together in the cabin, but I'm keeping my distance. I can't let myself fall for Caleb again.

Forced proximity only works in romance books. There's no way it'll work on us. Not if I stay strong and get through this until the snow clears.

CHAPTER 8
CALEB

Watching Holly eat the meal I made her is everything. I'm fixated on every sigh of enjoyment and muted squeal she thinks she's hiding from me. She can't fool me. I know her happy food dance when I see it.

"You like it?" I ask affectionately.

My fork hovers halfway to my mouth because I'm too entranced by her lips and the way her lashes flutter with each bite. I'm torn between scooting my stool at the island closer to hers to feel her nearness or staying put to enjoy the full view.

Holly pauses her delighted wriggling and swallows. "I mean, it's only the basics. It's not hard to make."

An amused huff escapes me. That mouthy demeanor of hers is addictive. I can't get enough.

"Everything made with love tastes better, right? Even the simplest meal," I say.

She rolls her eyes and reaches up to pat my head. I duck so it's easier for her with our height difference and enjoy the attention, no matter how sarcastically doled out.

"Yes, good boy."

Does she want me to bark? I'll bark for her.

I miss her touch as soon as it disappears.

I planned to spend my time at the cabin alone, yet I'm glad that expectation went out the window. The blizzard is a blessing in disguise in more ways than one for me. Yeah, it's given me the perfect way to lay low from sports media. But it also put me together with her.

From the moment I got here—hell, from the moment Holly took a swing at me with her rolling pin—one thing's become clear to me. This is my second chance to win her back.

I didn't realize it at twenty when I was so hungry to reach the big leagues in my hockey career. I know better now: Holly is the one who got away.

I screwed things up with her once and allowed her to slip through my fingers. I won't make that mistake again.

She might hate me now. I don't blame her. It's not like we've kept in touch. She stopped responding to any of my messages after summer break ended and I returned to campus at Heston U.

As far as I can tell from every mention of her when I'm

talking to Layla, and the late nights I've missed her so much I visited her social media profiles to see what she's up to, there's no one else right now.

My grip strangles my fork at the thought of her falling for anyone else, guy or girl. Layla mentioned Holly had a girlfriend right after college, but they didn't last. I don't think there's been other guys.

Since I entered professional hockey, my life has been dedicated to the game more than ever. Except after achieving the position I strived hard to reach, something was missing...*her.*

Maybe I was supposed to get dropped from my team. Maybe I was meant to find my way back to Holly to face everything I've regretted that held me back in the past.

This is my chance to fix it. To win her back.

No matter what it takes. Because she's the piece of my life I've been missing. The hollow space that I can't fill without her.

This time I can't let her walk away again—I won't.

My attention slips from her to the falling snow outside the window. It's slowed somewhat, though it's still coming down at a steady rate. I will it to last long enough to prove to her we should get back together.

Holly makes another stifled moan that steals my entire focus.

She freezes in the middle of licking her fork clean,

caught out. Her cheeks flush a pretty shade of pink as lovely as her cotton candy colored hair.

My hooded gaze locks on her plush lips. Fuck, I want to kiss her.

Need pulls at me, hot and insistent, igniting my arousal.

I want to sweep everything off the island counter so it crashes to the floor and spread her out on it. I need that moan from her again, without restraint.

"I'm glad you're enjoying what I made for you," I rasp.

She sputters, dropping her fork with a clatter. "Thanks for cooking. I'm done now. Put the dishes in the sink and I'll wash them after I shower."

After the tumble of words, she scampers in a cute shuffle of her slippers to bolt for the stairs. I prop my head with my hand, a slow smile curving my mouth. When I'm done eating, I clean everything up and wash the dishes so she doesn't have to worry about it.

I can't do this with obvious plays. It'll take a damn good deke and some tricky maneuvers to skate my way back into her heart. First I have to warm her up, make her think she's winning.

And to do that, I'll make sure I anticipate her needs, whatever they may be.

In the late afternoon, I come in from checking on Greta's water level. Cell service connected for about five minutes when I happened to check my phone. Holly immediately sent her brother several texts she had drafted in her phone notes. I had long enough to touch base with my family's group chat and let Jim know where his goose was before my signal dropped.

Holly's still in the kitchen where she's spent most of the day with her hair tied up in a bun by a shiny green bow, surrounded by baking ingredients. She's wearing a pink apron with frosted Christmas tree cakes printed all over it. Two more hang from the hooks on the wall, both with bold colors and patterns. The standing mixer she brought with her matches her hair color.

The sight of her in her element causes my chest to expand with a warm, bright sensation. I rub at my heart after it skips a beat because she looks up at me.

"Hey." I saunter to the kitchen.

"How's Greta?"

"She's good. What are you up to?"

She gives me a deadpan look and gestures at everything she's pulled out with a whisk that has a clear glitter handle. "Obviously, I'm setting up a seance to contact the great beyond."

I chuckle. "Badass."

She ducks her head to hide a smile. "Shut up."

"Make me," I fire back, letting my tone go low and suggestive.

Her wide-eyed expression flies to me. After floundering for a response, she lands on a chiding, "Caleb."

I tilt my head with a seductive hum. "Love it when you say my name, sugar cookie."

"*Caleb.*"

"That's it, baby. Keep saying it. You make it sound so nice." I jump away with a snicker when she tosses a handful of flour at me in retaliation. "Okay, you win. Truce."

I keep quiet for a few minutes so she doesn't chase me out of the kitchen. After I sweep the flour that fell on the floor, I post up on the other side of the island to watch. She swats at me when I pick up a can of fancy cocoa powder to read the label.

"I forgot to ask, but did you rob a grocery store on your way here?"

"No, this is all stuff I had at my place. Bakery owner, remember?" She points at herself with her whisk.

The edge of my mouth curls. "I remember. What are you making?"

"None of your business." She ignores me, going as far as turning her back to tune me out.

"That's fine if you don't want to share any with me," I tease. "I was just curious. You've always been so good at it. I like having the chance to watch you work up close."

"You'll make me self conscious. I'll probably get the recipe wrong for the first time ever because you're hovering," she throws over her shoulder.

The tips of her ears have turned red. It's cute how easily she gets flustered.

"I'll just start guessing. Let's see." I survey the flour, eggs, and brown sugar. "Cake."

"No." She scoots around me to grab butter.

"Brownies." I rub my stomach, getting hungry.

"Nope." This time there's a hint of humor in her voice.

Good. She's enjoying the game. I pretend to think, pushing up the sleeves of my sweater and bracing my arms on the island. She pauses what she's doing with parchment paper to sneak a look at my forearms from the corner of her eye.

"Pie?" I suggest.

"Try again," she answers airily, nudging the ginger in front of me.

"Whatever it is, I know it'll be delicious because you made it."

Holly huffs without any heat. "Cookies. It's not Christmas without homemade gingerbread cookies." She hesitates, toying with the bow in her hair. "Do you want to try? You can bake with me."

I hum in agreement. "Show me how."

She pats her standing mixer. "This baby handled most of the work. I already made one batch of dough earlier that should be ready to bake by now. I'm mixing up one more batch. Grab the dough from the fridge."

I do as she instructs, finding two thick hunks of cookie dough in the fridge. She has the dough coming together in the mixer faster than I expect while I'm still searching for the edge of the plastic wrap to get the first one open. She bumps my hip with hers and trades me for the newly wrapped dough when it's finished.

"Here, put this in there to chill."

"That was fast."

She scrunches her face in thought. "I've made about... seventy batches of these between my cookie orders and the shop's regular menu in the last few weeks. I can do this in my sleep."

"Impressive," I praise.

Whenever I compliment her, she's like a flower seeking the sun, basking in it.

"Okay. Now the fun part—rolling and cutting out our shapes," she says.

Holly starts a holiday playlist on her phone. She gives me her rolling pin, then rifles through the drawer for the old one that's been here for ages. After she gives a quick demonstration, we get to work. She makes it look easy, even with a battered tool.

"You want to go back and forth so it spreads evenly. Long strokes," she advises, watching my clumsy technique.

I can't help the innuendo my mind turns her wisdom into. "Yeah? Long, hard strokes?"

Her tongue clicks and she rolls her eyes sardonically. "Not too hard."

"Mm, no." I chuckle. "Hang on. How are you getting yours all nice like that?"

"Like this."

She covers my hands with hers to teach me. I'm not paying attention to the dough anymore, too occupied with her.

The feel of her fingers curled around mine makes me swallow thickly. She has no idea how her simple touch is on the brink of sending me to my knees.

Our eyes lock. I hold her attention, not hiding the longing in my stare. My heart thuds, hard and persistent.

She licks her lips and averts her gaze. When she's satisfied, she nods.

"That's good. Take your pick of the cutters."

As we cut the shapes, we continue trading banter. Spending time with her like this brings me immeasurable enjoyment.

We get our cookies into the oven to bake once they're ready. It smells amazing and I'm looking forward to trying them.

The timer goes off ten minutes later. I admire her ass when she bends to pull out the trays, swallowing an appreciative groan.

"What's next?" I eat the scrap pieces of cookie dough.

She snags one from me with a sly expression and pops it in her mouth. "Making icing."

I get out of her way as she whips it up. Whenever she's not looking, I keep stealing some with my finger.

"Oh my god, you're unstoppable." She giggles, wrestling the bowl from me. "Stop eating it all, or we won't have any to decorate with."

I wind an arm around Holly's middle, tugging her back against my chest. "One more taste. I'm not above putting you in air jail to get it. I might be a professional athlete, but I'm still human. Sometimes a man just wants a sweet treat."

If I could have her, that would be an even better one.

Her shoulders shake with laughter. It's infectious.

"We're making the sweet treat still. Be patient." She holds the bowl overhead like it will do anything to keep it away from me.

"Did you forget I'm a foot taller than you?" I swipe it from her.

"Hey!" She hops on the tips of her toes to get it back.

I push my advantage, drawing her in by her waist and setting the icing aside. "Got you."

Her breath hitches and she stares at me. My thumb caresses her lower back and her hands fall to rest on my shoulders.

Time stretches and every one of my nerve endings come alive with awareness of her.

How she subtly presses into me, possibly oblivious she's shifting closer. Her throat constricting with a swallow. The parting of her lips. Her blue eyes, as sparkling as everything else about her, bouncing back and forth between mine.

I dip my head a fraction, intent on capturing those lips for the taste I really want. My face hovers close to hers, letting her decide how this goes. She licks her lips, peering up at me with desire in her gaze.

Holly speaks in a hush. "They should be cooled enough to decorate now."

"Alright," I answer, equally soft.

My fingers curl into my palms after she steps away, memorizing how it felt to hold her.

The game isn't won with one strategy. I'm in it for as many plays as it takes to break down her walls.

After flitting around the kitchen for a minute with a rosy blush, she sets up a station for each of us with a tray of our gingerbread and skillfully prepares piping bags with icing. Her passion for baking is clear even now as we make something just because. For as long as I've conditioned my hockey technique, she's been fine tuning hers as a baker.

A rush of pride fills my chest to see how far she's come from the girl I grew up with who was running bake sales and watching every dessert cooking show.

"What's your expert tips on doing this?" I gesture with the icing bag, tempted to squirt some directly in my mouth.

She shrugs. "Just go with whatever you're feeling. Baking is supposed to be fun. No pressure, okay?"

"Like this?" I draw an abstract smiley face and give my gingerbread man a hilariously large dick.

Holly smothers a snicker. "Beautifully done."

She shows me up by decorating three cookies for every one I finish. Her artistry clearly marks her the professional here, even when she gives hers nice sets of boobs with heart-shaped nipples. She finishes them with a flourish, smirking at her creation.

"Put on a pair of skates and hit the ice with me. I want to see if you do this well in my area of expertise," I challenge.

She narrows her eyes playfully. "You're on."

After we get through them all with me chirping at her and her heckling me right back, I'm unable to wipe a grin off my face. There's no trace of the worried knots that contorted my insides before I arrived. She's loosened them all.

"Damn, that's good," I say at the first bite of the cookie.

"It's my recipe tweak. I like to keep them more moist and give them more of a caramel flavor than when you use typical molasses and brown sugar ratios." She looks like she's in heaven nibbling on her treat. "I'm making some hot cocoa to go with these."

"Sounds good." I get the dishes started.

She pauses what she's doing. When I glance at her, she's staring at me like I've given her the world by cleaning up before she had the chance.

Something warm and nice flickers in my stomach that makes me want to do anything to make her feel like she can rely on me to ease her burdens.

"I've got this," I say easily.

She bites her lip. "Thanks."

"What do you want for dinner tonight?"

"It's my turn," she argues. "You made breakfast and our lunch."

"And I'm cooking dinner, too."

"But—"

"Nope. I'm taking care of it."

Of you.

She slides her lips together and her brows wrinkle as if she doesn't know why I would. Like no one ever offers. I want to cradle her face, soothe her plush lower lip with my thumb, and reassure her she deserves the world. And I will give it to her.

"Alright. I appreciate it," she murmurs.

"Once you're done with the cocoa, you go relax," I encourage. "This is supposed to be your vacation."

She rolls her lips between her teeth, then breaks into a beaming smile. "Okay, deal."

The pleasant sensation in my chest expands. I dry my hands on the dish towel and lean against the sink to appreciate her happiness as she dances to the holiday music playing in the background.

It's clear to me now Holly is always used to being the one who takes care of everyone else around her without anyone to do the same for her.

Time to change that, because she has me to take care of her. And when I dedicate myself to something, I put my all into it.

CHAPTER 9
HOLLY

CHOPPING firewood is way harder than it looks. It seems like a straightforward process. Place wood. Take aim. Chop.

I figured this would be therapeutic and easy. Instead, it's pissing me off more than it's providing any outlet for stress relief.

Actually, the true reason I'm so worked up is because of Caleb.

For three days in a row, he's gotten up earlier than me —a surprise all on its own considering the first morning here he practically sleepwalked straight into my tits—and made breakfast for me every morning.

And lunch.

And dinner.

Hell, he's even preparing snacks in between meals. He

made me a goddamn cheese board. How am I supposed to resist cheese?

A man who keeps a woman fed is a unicorn these days.

Is it the bare minimum? Of course, but this is a man I'm talking about. They're so different from dating women. Although, my relationship with the girl I dated after college fell apart, too. The few dates I've been on since haven't gone further than the first few outings, and none progressed to the relationship stage because no one measured up to someone who deserves me.

The important barometer here is *if he wanted to, he would.*

And Caleb is pulling out all the stops without leaving any room to wonder his motive.

The coffee is brewed exactly how I like it each morning by the time I'm awake, and after we eat he doesn't allow me to lift a finger to help him do the dishes. When I insisted I should do my share of chores since he keeps cooking, he said he remembered that washing dishes is one of my most disliked tasks ever and he didn't mind doing them for me if it makes my life easier, leaving me speechless.

I'm not blind. He's not hiding those alluring looks or how his gaze turns sultry and hooded at the lingering touches whenever our hands brush.

I'm not immune to his charming efforts, either.

When he nearly kissed me a few nights ago, I almost let him.

The resolution I made to withstand his charisma, no matter how tempting? Completely forgotten once I was trapped by those irresistible green eyes, shivering from him being near enough his breath ghosted across my mouth.

I was so swept up in how fun it was to bake with him. He's always been a good kisser and it's been too long since I was last kissed until I was melting. The last person to kiss me like that was him.

I was moments from slipping my arms around his broad, sturdy shoulders and tilting my chin up, anticipating his mouth claiming mine.

The fantasy of what could've been flashes in my mind.

How he'd hover his lips over mine and ask if I wanted him to kiss me.

How I'd whisper *yes*.

His embrace tightening and the relieved groan that might slip out of him before his mouth collided with mine in a sizzling kiss full of the passion we once burned with together.

I press my chilled fingers to my lips and close my eyes before fantasy Caleb lifts me by my waist to the counter and fits his sexy sculpted body between my thighs.

I want to stay mad at him and hold on to my grudge forever. Yet he's finding every possible way to get under my skin by being so doting. I swear, before I even realize I need something, he seems to anticipate it.

Whether it's bringing me a blanket and a mug of hot cocoa while I'm reading by the fire, warming my towel before I shower, or cleaning up for me after I spend hours baking—he thoughtfully sees to everything little I could want without being asked.

He's tempting me to risk it all by letting my guard down. It's difficult to thwart when he comes across as a far more grown up and earnest version of himself than the driven boy who left to become a professional hockey player. Trouble is...if I did, would we be repeating our short-lived indulgence only for him to pick hockey over me again?

Why does it have to be him my heart is so smitten with? It doesn't matter that I'm attracted to more than one gender, no one has ever made it beat as strongly as he does.

Normally in this precarious situation I'd ask Layla for her advice, but going to my best friend about her brother is out of the question. The thrill of sneaking around because we were young and impulsive made us keep things a secret before. When things ended before we got serious, I ended up not telling Layla, struck by how ridiculous I was for catching feelings over a fling.

I miss her, though. We rarely go more than forty-eight hours without talking. The cell signal is still spotty since it stopped snowing two days ago, and after checking in with my brother first, I only manage to chat with Layla for short spurts before it drops.

At least Leo called Hazel down to Mayfield to help him and Leta manage things at Blissful Bites while I'm gone. They've all promised me they're going to take good care of my baby.

The blizzard might be over, but it left everything buried under heaps of fresh snow. We're still stuck here until the roads are cleared.

Since Caleb took care of cooking, *again*, I thought I'd pay him back by chopping more firewood so we're even.

I'm getting nowhere with it. The best I managed was splintering a piece that's little more than kindling. I keep missing or getting the axe stuck partway down the log before it cuts all the way through.

The thought of asking Caleb for his help crosses my mind.

I hastily chase the urge away. Not only because I don't want to admit defeat, but also because asking for *anyone's* help is difficult for me. It makes me feel like I'm making a burden of myself. I figure things out on my own, the way I always have. It's faster and far easier than opening myself up for the chance to be let down.

Raising the axe overhead, I squint at my target and let it have it with a fierce yell.

I think I've got it this time. The swing felt good and I connected with the wood. Except to my dismay, the blade is stuck halfway through the log I've been chipping away at.

"Ugh. Me and wood are not getting along up here."

It takes some struggling and planting my foot on the log to remove the axe. When it pops free, I stumble backwards, catching myself before I plant my ass in a snowbank Caleb shoveled a path through so we could walk to the wood pile. He hasn't cleared the massive amounts of snow engulfing our cars yet.

After blowing loose strands of pink hair from my face, I grip the handle hard enough to choke and prop my fists on my hips. While the logical side of my brain understands that every skill takes practice to achieve the desired end result, it really irritates me when I'm not immediately good at something.

A judgmental honk from Greta makes me laugh and hang my head back.

Once the storm was over, Caleb hiked the two miles and back to get her home to the farm, but she's returned today. She parked her fluffy white goose butt nearby when I started my attempts to chop wood.

"You're not helping," I tell her.

She preens her feathers with a distinct cluck that I can only interpret as her giving me attitude.

"Keep it up and you're cut off from my cranberries," I warn.

The goose ignores me, helping herself to the berries I

brought out for her when she appeared out of the pine trees. As I get ready for chopping attempt number...I've lost count, she wanders off around the bushes.

"You can do this," I coach. "Line it up where you want to hit it. Picture it's Caleb's head. His inflated, infuriatingly attractive face."

I swing and wedge it right into the same spot I got stuck in before. This time it's not budging when I tug the handle.

"Oh, come on," I say with a sigh.

"Need my help?"

I whirl around at the deep, smoky offer to find Caleb leaning a shoulder against the porch column with a mug set on the railing in front of him. He's watching me with the hint of a smirk, arms folded. He's the picture of a casual, laid-back mountain man. I do my best to ignore how nice his muscled arms look pulling his sweater taut.

"How long have you been there?" I ask.

"Only a minute." His eyes dance with humor and satisfaction. "My face is attractive, huh?"

"No," I snap too quickly.

His grin spreads slowly. "Whatever you say, sugar cookie."

Greta's attitude changes immediately from dour to excited as she comes back from exploring. She cackles, flapping her wings and waddling to him. He meets her halfway, crouching with a fond, crooked smile.

"Hi, pretty girl." He strokes her back.

"Of course you want the heartbreaker," I mutter.

"Heartbreaker?" Caleb repeats.

I didn't mean for him to overhear the nickname I've been calling him by for years in my head. Crossing my arms, I lift my chin.

"Yeah. That's you."

"I see," he muses. "Well, we have to fix that. Don't we, Greta?"

He acts like it'll be so easy. As if he already knows his odds of getting into my pants is a done deal.

Cocky ass.

No matter how much he flirts with me, or makes me food, or acts all cool and swoonworthy—it's not happening. I have a perfectly working vibrator in my luggage. I don't need him.

I rest the axe against the stump and stretch. Despite not having much to show for it, my arms twinge from the workout.

"Come take a break, tough girl. I made you this to warm you up." He nods to the steaming mug he left on the railing.

My mouth purses to the side. I take him up on it, only because I'm cold.

Greta hisses in warning at my approach, arching her neck to stare me down with one eye. She puffs up her feathers to appear more intimidating.

I freeze. "Is she going to attack me?"

"I'd never let that happen. But she can be a little, uh... possessive of me, I guess." He covers his mouth, obviously hiding how hilarious he finds it.

This is what my life has come to. Beefing with a territorial goose that likes my ex-boyfriend better than me.

"Girl, you can have him," I say to the goose.

Muffled laughter escapes Caleb. "Ladies, ladies. No need to fight over me. Greta, you have to be a nice goose. We like Holly. We don't hiss at her."

Scoffing, I return to my pitiful excuse for chopping firewood. He lets me get one more swing in before he comes over to help me dislodge it.

His hands curl around mine and his chest is a solid force at my back. My breath hitches and I'm overwhelmed by his delicious woodsy, masculine scent. With his arms surrounding me, he frees it with a firm yank.

"Let me do this. Drink your coffee before it cools down," he says.

His tone carries a hint of authority that stirs molten heat low in my stomach. It leaves me short of breath with butterflies tickling my stomach.

My grip tightens on the axe because I'm hardwired to fight anyone who tries to tell me to do something out of stubbornness. He doesn't give it up yet, studying me tenderly.

"I'll do it for you," he says.

"I can do it myself," I shoot back.

"I know. But I want to take care of it for you so you don't wear yourself out."

My stomach flips. When he says things like that, my heart forgets why I shouldn't like him.

"Unless you want me to teach you?" He steps into me. "Show you how to hold it right? If that's what you want, say the word."

I release the handle with a sharp inhale at the innuendo and narrow my eyes. "I can't stand you."

He tilts his head, chuckling with a smug grin. "Is that right? I don't believe you."

Make that two of us. Because I'm not sure my own words are convincing when my heart is beating fast and being near him sparks excitement that races through me.

"Enjoy your coffee," he murmurs.

He guides me a few paces away with a hand resting at my lower back to keep me out of harm's way before he plants his feet and winds up.

With one swing that embodies the strength, grace, and coordination of the athlete he is, he splits the log I hacked at in two. Then he resets a piece and splinters it in half again, then another until it's whittled down to four pieces.

He makes it look effortless. And hot. Really fucking hot.

My mouth goes dry as he continues, hoisting up a bulky log like it weighs nothing at all to him before bringing the axe down with a masculine grunt. The crack of the wood coming apart where the axe strikes reverberates with a pang of desire inside me. The simmering, insistent pulse continues with each chop until I'm aching.

It's impossible to tear my attention from him.

As an eldest daughter, I'm as independent as they come. Yet part of me likes the ways he's taking care of me.

CHAPTER 10
CALEB

BEING TUCKED AWAY from the world is pure bliss. I'm enjoying the hell out of this. My concerns over my contract termination have been buried by every minute spent with Holly earning those mouthy retorts that drive me wild and testing all the ways to make her blush.

At least until I read the new messages from my family group chat. Cell service has become more reliable since early this morning when I almost put my phone through the wall to stop the alarm dragging me from sleep before dawn, then remembered my motivation for getting my ass out of bed before the sun's up.

I'm expecting another check in from my family. What I get instead is a link from my sister to a sports news site with a headline that reads *One Half of the Star Adler Brothers League Combo—Not Fit for the Culture?*

Fucking vultures. They're still at it?

The worst part of this is that no matter what, people will remember this about me. The fans. Whatever team I end up with in the future. Any staff within that organization.

Once an opinion hits the internet, it spreads like wildfire. Little can be done to douse those flames, and no one cares to know the true story when there's juicy drama to entertain them instead.

I don't bother clicking on the link. My brother's on damage control as the only one in my family I told the full truth to.

ELIJAH

Layla... [gravestone emoji]

MOM

What is this? You know your father and I don't like to see these nasty articles. They're fish bait.

ELIJAH

Clickbait, Mom. It's clickbait.

LAYLA

Wait. Shit. Wrong chat.

CALEB

Don't bother unsending it. I've already seen.

LAYLA

Sorry. I was texting it to Eli to ask what it meant.

I massage the bridge of my nose with a sigh. This is on me for not telling my family more details about the situation. All I explained to my parents and sister was that I'd been fired from my team and would be home for a while until Trevon strategizes my next steps as a free agent.

ELIJAH

It's bullshit, that's what it means. Ignore those fuckers.

CALEB

I was until someone gave me the holiday gift of shoving it in my face.

LAYLA

I'm sorryyy!

CALEB

Don't worry about it. They're all wrong anyway.

ELIJAH

Damn right they are. You've been offline, but fans across the whole league are pissed.

My stomach clenches. Does he mean they're mad at me? He's still typing. I thumb the edge of the phone as the three dots dance forever.

"Here, taste this. I can't decide if I want to make these for my winter menu or not." Holly appears at my shoulder from behind the couch with the desserts she's been baking all morning.

The uneasy tension in my stomach loosens and I can breathe again.

I grasp her wrist to bring the stuffed flaky pastry covered with nuts and a drizzle of caramel to my mouth for a bite. As it melts on my tongue with bursts of cinnamon and pecan, my gaze locks with hers. I groan appreciatively at the buttery rich flavor.

"Well? What are your thoughts?"

"Fuck, that's good." I keep hold of her wrist and go for another bite.

She licks her lips and looks away. "If you let go of my hand, I'll bring you a plate."

"Or you could feed the rest to me?" I waggle my brows and pat my lap. "This seat's not taken."

She scoffs. "Yeah? I could shove it down your throat in one go."

"Give it to me, baby." I open wide, shoulders shaking with suppressed amusement.

She crams most of the piece in my mouth and walks

off while I bend over to catch the rest, admiring the sway of her amazing curvy ass.

My brother's answer finally pops up in the family chat after I've downed it and picked the crumbs off my old college sweatshirt.

ELIJAH

You might not be able to say anything about the press release your team made glossing over the situation, but the girl you helped made a post on her social media. It's being shared everywhere. The truth will come out that you weren't beating up your teammate in a drunken bar brawl like they're trying to spin it. Word's already spreading amongst other plays in the league. All the guys on my team are just as pissed for you.

DAD

What's this got to do with a girl?

CALEB

One of my younger teammates was putting his hands on her when she was saying no. I put an end to it.

DAD

I see. I'm proud of you for doing the right thing, son. What does this have to do with you leaving the team?

CALEB

The kid's family has money and swept it all under the rug. I got the boot because the media was already reporting about the fight he started with me for stepping in.

MOM

That's horrible. It isn't right.

LAYLA

Wow, what the hell? How can they get away with that?

ELIJAH

Money is power.

LAYLA

I hate this.

CALEB

It fucking sucks, but just ignore the media and don't talk to anyone weird that emails or calls you. Trevon's got it handled for me and so does his legal team. I don't want to play for a team that keeps a piece of trash like Chet on their roster, anyway.

LAYLA

True. I'm gonna make a fake account to troll him hard.

I read a text Elijah sends me separately from the group chat saying he'll personally pull a penalty against Chet at his game scheduled against Seattle after the Christmas break. A smirk twists my lips. The baby brother who followed after me in everything my entire life all the way to the NHL is the one fighting my battles now.

Ready to retreat back to my bubble with Holly, I shut the world out again by pushing my phone between the couch cushions. My attention shifts to her dancing around the kitchen and writing notes on her tablet.

I amble over and brace my hands on the island next to her. She doesn't look up from writing a note on the sketch of one of her pastries on her tablet.

"You've been baking up a storm," I say.

"You know, at first I thought this sucked. I don't like sitting still and being snowed in feels like I'm trapped in place. But actually?" She stops writing to turn a beaming expression on me that steals my breath. "This isn't so bad. I'm getting so much work done! Usually I squeeze the seasonal menu changes in between custom orders or late at night. But I planned out the entire next year!"

"Impressive. If you're ahead, we should get out of here," I suggest.

She laughs as she swipes through her sketched recipes. "And go where? The cars are out of commission still. I don't think we'd get far on foot."

"When I was clearing out the shed for Greta, I found the old sleds." I squeeze her shoulders and give her a teasing shake. "What do you say? Race me down the hill like we used to?"

She slumps against me, sighing nostalgically at the idea of playing in the snow. "God, I haven't been sledding in years. I was going to start making ideas for the cookie orders waiting in my inbox, though."

The strong desire to wrap her in my arms and hold her slams into me. If I do, I might never stop hugging her.

"It's your vacation. You can't work the whole way through, or it defeats the purpose." I bring my lips to her ear and murmur encouragingly. "It's okay to take a break, sugar. Come outside in the snow with me."

Her breath hitches and she shivers. Peeking over her shoulder through her lashes, she smiles.

"Okay. But I'm totally beating you."

Warm laughter rolls out of me. "We'll see about that. Go check the closet upstairs for Layla's spare snow clothes. I'll get the sleds ready."

CHAPTER 11
HOLLY

An exhilarated scream bursts from me as my sled careens down the slope behind the cabin. It echoes off the treetops. I feel so free. More than I have in forever.

Caleb's sled isn't far behind me. He yelps with a curse as we reach the bottom, crashing out while I slide to victory over the finish line we marked with two sticks for our sled racing.

Laughter bubbles out of me as I coast to a stop in a thick snowdrift near the frozen pond at the bottom of the hill. I tumble off the sled and pump my arms and legs in the air.

"I win again!"

Caleb drags his sled to my side and leans over me. "Rematch."

"We can go again and again, I'll still win," I taunt

while making a snow angel. "Face it, you don't have what it takes, big guy. All that muscle slows you down. I'm the reigning champion of this hill."

He tongues his cheek and nods wryly. "It's sledding. There's not much to it."

"Says the sore loser who choked at the end of the race," I goad with a snicker.

"You and that competitive streak," he says affectionately.

I take the hand he gives me to stand up, holding on to my hat. He adjusts it for me so it covers my ears again, then dusts the snow off my coat.

"Having a good time?"

"Surprisingly, yes. I forgot how much fun this is."

"Are you warm enough?"

His hands rest on my upper arms and he caresses them absently with his thumbs. I catch myself enjoying his attentive concern for me.

"Yeah. The coat you gave me is toasty."

My bust size and curvier hips are more generous than Layla's old ski clothes from high school. Since I couldn't fit into them anymore, I'm bundled in his instead.

"Good." He scoops up some snow and forms it into a ball in his gloved hands. "Because now it's payback time for kicking my ass, you little speed queen."

"Wait—wait!" Shrieking with another bout of laughter, I jump out of the way of the snowball he throws. "Oh, it's on!"

I hastily retaliate, ducking from his onslaught. My stomach hurts from laughing so hard. He chases me all over the clearing surrounding the pond, both of us cracking up.

Running through the deep snow is hard, but I dive behind a tree before he fires off the next one. Making as many snowballs as I can, I start flinging them at him. Two hit him in succession, one in the chest and one in the knee.

"Yes!"

I have just enough time for a victory dance before he rushes me. He captures me in his strong embrace.

"Gotcha."

"Oh no you don't." I wriggle, attempting to trip him.

His arms tighten and he swings me off my feet. Through the layers of our clothes, the deep reverberation of his lighthearted laughter fills me with happiness.

This is the most carefree I've been in a long time. No worries or responsibilities can touch me.

Our play wrestling ends up making both of us fall when we overbalance. He catches me and breaks my fall, holding me as I land on his chest.

"You okay?" He rubs my back.

"Yeah."

I stare at him, my gaze flickering between his eyes. His green irises are mesmerizing, full of tender reverence. A tingle runs down my spine as I go still, laughter fading. The playful mood shifts and warmth spreads through me. My heartbeat skips, my breathing quickening as butterflies dance around inside me.

Something intangible and electric sparks between us. A shiver races across my skin that has nothing to do with the cold outdoors.

He holds me tighter when my attention falls to his mouth. I lick my lips and he stifles a strained noise at the back of his throat. His body is firm beneath me, yet the solid muscle mass brings me so much comfort. I feel safest when he holds me.

Without realizing it, I've leaned closer, drawn in by an invisible magnetism.

My nose brushes his. He exhales shakily, clutching the oversized coat I borrowed from him.

Is that his heart drumming loudly, or mine?

I want to whisper his name, but I'm afraid to speak. Every part of me is strung taut, quivering with an unspoken desire to give in and kiss him.

At the last second, I grow flustered and shove snow down his neck instead to break the tension. I scramble off him while he's writhing with a shocked bark from the cold.

In my hurry to get away, I stumble in the snow. Crumpling in a heap, my face scrunches as pain twinges in my ankle.

"Crap—ow!"

"Are you okay?" Caleb's voice is laced with concern.

He comes to my aid, tugging off a glove with his teeth and smoothing his palm over my leg. I wince when he helps me roll it gently.

He watches me with a worried frown. "Sorry. I just want to make sure you didn't break it."

"I think I twisted it. Not that bad."

I try to get up and he stops me. "Take it easy. Let me check you over before you stand on it."

"Okay."

I only agree because being cared for by someone else gratifies a deep, hidden part of me that I've wrapped under armor I've spent a lifetime fortifying.

His handsome features set in concentration as he gingerly prods and massages my ankle. The fleeting pain fades with his attentive treatment. I sigh in relief, indulging in his dedication and, secretly, his touch.

"It feels a lot better now," I say.

"I think you're good. Just strained the muscle. Let's head back so you can rest it."

He helps me to my feet, supporting me even as I insist I'm fine. We leave the sleds behind for now, going slow. I stretch my leg and test how it feels. It aches slightly, but feels like it'll be better within a few hours.

At the base of the hill leading up to the cabin, I pause, not looking forward to the climb with a sore ankle. Caleb steps in front of me.

"Hop up."

He hunches low to make up for our height difference. I stare at his back, not making a move to take the offer.

"You're serious?"

He chuckles and shoots a grin at me.

"Yeah. Are you hopping up on my back or am I tossing you over my shoulder instead?"

Damn it. I'm a simple girl. All I want is to be tossed around and kept well-fed.

Caleb's checking boxes he's not supposed to.

I slide my arms around his shoulders. He grips my legs and lifts me so effortlessly, I cling to him in surprise. He starts up the slope without complaint.

Unable to resist, I snuggle against him, resting my chin on his shoulder.

"You're going to carry me the whole way back?" I ask.

"Of course I will." He squeezes my legs. "I've got you. Always will."

I bite my lip, heart beating harder.

"It's uphill. I'm not exactly light. It's too much—"

"You're not too much, Holly. Nothing about you is. Anyone who makes you think that will have to answer to me."

The fierce conviction in Caleb's tone pierces the hardest parts of my defensive walls, sending a wave of something warm and soft spreading throughout my chest.

He holds on tighter, unwilling to let me down. "You

know, I'm not a guy that trains hard at the gym just to play hockey in peak condition. I do it so I can carry my girl whenever I want, because this is exactly what I was made for. Carrying you whenever you need me to."

I'm not your girl anymore. I want to say it out of habit, but I hold the thought in as my emotions threaten to bubble over from my watering eyes.

His grip flexes and his voice becomes gruff, edged with something that sounds jealous. "Anyone you've dated since is a fucking joke if they don't want to be the one holding you up. That'll never be me. I just want to take care of you."

He doesn't seriously mean what he's saying...does he? I'm struck with the force of how badly I want to believe him because being stuck alone in the cabin with him has brought everything rushing back from the place I buried it deep inside me.

My heart climbs into my throat, making it hard to swallow past the lump forming. "Does that mean I have to answer to you?"

He makes a questioning noise. I blow out a breath, tucking my face into his shoulder to muffle myself.

"What if I'm the one who thinks I'm too much?"

Caleb stops and kneads my thighs reassuringly. His voice softens with a caring gentleness that's a balm to the ache of self doubt in my chest.

"Holly, you're amazing. Not only do you run your own

bakery you started all on your own, your talent and passion for what you do are unmatched. You're sweet, kind, and generous. You're always worrying about everyone else first before yourself."

He speaks with such fervent confidence in his words, I'm left speechless. But he's not done yet, continuing in a hoarse, almost desperate plea.

"Everyone you meet sees that about you. *I* see you. Believe me, not any voice in your head."

My eyes widen and my mouth falls open. "Caleb, I…"

"I'm serious. Don't put yourself down," he says quietly.

"I don't, not really. Sometimes it just crosses my mind."

He cranes his neck to see me. "Then I'll just need to stick around to always chase away your doubts when that happens."

An arrow of profound longing pierces through me. It's everything I wish he would've promised me before I ended things between us. What I hoped he would've fought for when I started ignoring his messages and calls, leaving me to believe I was right about our summer fling.

I slide my lips together to keep myself from crying, touched and clinging to the raw emotions he's stirred up in me. I feel a little silly to get so choked up over him being nice to me, yet he's met a need I wasn't aware I direly craved.

"You okay? You went quiet on me," he murmurs.

"Yeah." I sniffle, hoping he thinks my nose is running from the icy temperature.

"The Caleb express is leaving the station. Everyone keep your arms and legs safely tucked against the vehicle at all times. Groping is encouraged," he jokes.

I hide a husky laugh in his neck. "Thank you."

"Anytime, sugar. Anything for you."

Unlike the whirlwind summer we spent sneaking around years ago...I do believe him this time.

He's different now. Still a charismatic flirt with a laid-back personality, yet he's grown into himself. He's more mature and someone I could easily fall for again.

The real reason I'm afraid of these reawakening feelings for Caleb is because I don't want to be hurt like I was in the past.

I was more invested in us than he was, so when I overheard his coach warning him about focusing on his athletics I pushed away first so I could protect my heart. It still broke anyway when he didn't chase after me.

If I fall for him a second time, I could be left behind again when he returns to his life as a hockey star.

Yet I can't help it. It's too late. He's already slipping past my defenses and finding his way back into my heart.

There's no way to get him out of it. And for the first time since we've been stuck together...I don't think I want to.

CHAPTER 12
CALEB

TOMORROW MARKS a week since we've been snowed in. With one week left until Christmas, I don't know how much longer I have to win Holly's heart before the roads are cleared. I thought I came close the few times when we've almost kissed, but she's holding back.

I'm not afraid to work for it. She's worth it in every way.

My skates carve smoothly through the ice on the frozen pond. I found one of my old sticks in the storage shed and a game puck I'd forgotten was in my equipment bag. Muscle memory takes over as I circle the makeshift rink.

My lips tug into a wry smirk when I consider the state of the art arena I was skating in last week. Instead of the sick twist of my stomach, I'm relaxed. It's nice to just skate for once. I can't remember the last time I just chilled like this.

Once my legs are warmed up, I flick a wrister to an imaginary goal. It's a beauty, lighting the lamp in my head when it soars into the net. I retrieve the puck and line up another shot on my makeshift goal line.

The whoop I let out echoes off the treetops. I forgot this freedom that made me fall in love with the game in the first place.

The reason I'm in such good spirits has a lot to do with news I got from my agent early this morning while I was cooking something special for my girl before she woke up.

Trevon was surprised I answered the phone. I took his ball busting and pressed him about the teams he's been talking to. I nearly dropped the cranberry cornbread skillet I was putting in the oven when he grimly said the Metropolitan and Atlantic Division teams were lowballing offers. He put me out of my misery as he continued, letting me know he got a surprising call from an old teammate of his who wants a meeting.

It's not officially announced yet, but there's a new team being developed to join the NHL based in Massachusetts. And they're interested in me.

Sports news has been speculating about a league expansion with an increase in teams over the next few years. Me and a lot of the guys I know in the league have been following the possibility with interest.

Trevon wouldn't tell me any more than the bare bones, but he's hooked my curiosity. As soon as the roads on the mountain are open, I'll be ready to set up a meeting.

I speed up, driving the puck down the side of the pond. In my head, I'm in a brand new jersey with a second chance at glory. An unseen crowd cheers as I close in on the net and slam the puck in with a slap shot.

There's no doubt in my mind. I've got more to give. To the game. To myself. To the people most important to me in my life.

I'm feeling good about what lies ahead for me. Much better than I was boarding the flight from Seattle believing I was abruptly leaving my professional hockey career behind, cut off on a sour note that tarnished everything I poured into it.

Except there's something I want more than getting back on NHL ice.

Holly by my side.

I won't leave the cabin regretting the life we could have together for another seven years of radio silence. Not when I have her back now. I'm holding on to her, and I won't ever let her go again.

If I thought she'd accept without thinking I was being wildly impulsive, I'd get down on one knee and put my ring on her finger right now.

The future I want with her as my wife flashes through my head. Playing hockey knowing she's rooting for me. Being at her bakery to watch in awe of her in her element. Dedicating myself to caring for her in every way she needs. I crave all of it, as long as it's with her.

As if thinking about how much I want her summons her, I loop around to find her watching from the edge of the pond. The warmth expanding in my chest whenever I have her attention is becoming familiar again. I can't get enough of it.

The ends of the bow in her hair blow in the breeze. She's wearing pink pajama pants with Christmas cookies printed on them stuffed into her boots. Best of all, she borrowed my hoodie. Damn, it looks great. I like seeing her bundled in my clothes.

Waving with a grin, I show off for her.

I pull out all my slickest moves, speeding across the ice like I'm evading defense. She chirps like the best of the fans at first.

"You call that hockey? My grandma plays better than that," she calls.

My mouth tilts and I skate by her with a wink, blowing her a kiss. "You want to see something? I'll give you something to cheer about."

"Oh yeah? That's some big talk." She bites her lip, her blue eyes sparkling with amusement.

"Watch me."

I give her my finest skating, flipping backwards, crossing over, passing the puck between my legs and bouncing it off my blades. She forgets she was teasing me and gets into it.

"Go, go, score! Yes!" She bounces in celebration when I hit the puck and it zooms into the imaginary net.

I can't help picturing what it would be like to have her at my games. If I hadn't let her slip through my fingers and she'd been with me my whole career.

Knowing she's watching me, cheering for me. Dedicating every goal to her. Kissing her on the ice after we win.

Her wearing my jersey. My number. My *name*.

My head swims from how strongly I want all those things with her. I close my eyes and blow out a breath to weather the force of my desire for her.

"Okay, I admit it. You looked really cool doing that," Holly says.

Soft laughter escapes me. Coming to a stop near her, I lean on my stick and run my fingers through my hair.

"Want to skate with me?"

She brightens. "That sounds fun."

I duck my face with a broad smile. "I brought a spare pair with me in case you came down. Here, sit on my bag and I'll help you put them on."

Setting aside my stick and puck, I crouch at her feet and tug off her shoes. She wrinkles her toes against the chill. I rub them to warm her up. She blushes, darting her gaze to the side when I glance up. The urge to keep touching her simmers in my gut, tempting me to slide a hand up to stroke her calves.

After I've laced her skates, I take her hand and help her keep her balance stepping onto the frozen pond. She wobbles, clutching me when I catch her waist.

"I've got you," I promise.

"I can't remember the last time I went ice skating," she muses. "I feel like I've got fawn legs and any second I'll wipe out. How did this used to be so easy?"

"Confidence is the key. Muscle memory comes second," I answer.

"Okay, Mister I Wear Sharp Knife Boots and fly around the ice at top speed for a living. Easy for you to say," she jibes as we make slow progression.

"You can do it. I won't let you fall."

"You swear you'll catch me?"

Her grip on my hand tightens. I squeeze back.

"Always."

She trusts me and allows herself to relax enough to find her rhythm. I match my pace to hers. We fall into sync together as we circle the pond.

"Better?" I ask.

"Yeah. Now I'm getting the hang of it again."

"Should I leave hockey behind so we can register as pairs skaters?" I tease.

She scoffs out a laugh. "What? No. Be serious. I'm born to bake, and there's not a soul in the world who would believe you weren't born to do anything but play hockey." She bumps her hip against mine. "You can see it all over your face when you're on the ice, you know. How much you obviously love it."

"Yeah?" The swell in my chest makes me feel like I could soar hearing her say that.

"Although you looked like you were having more fun just messing around on the pond than the last few times I've caught recaps of your games," she muses.

I jerk to a stop. "You've seen them?"

A caught out expression crosses her face and her cheeks flush. I try to tamp down on the flood of emotion strong enough to knock me over, shock and elation fighting to win out.

"Um, yes," she replies with a rueful chuckle. "I've... sort of been following you as a player the whole time. Oh, god, this is embarrassing to confess, but what the hell. I have an alert on my phone for hockey news just so I could keep up with you."

My world shatters and rearranges.

This whole time—the nights I've spent in hotel rooms, on team flights, in my own empty bed rereading the old texts we've sent each other wishing I could reach out to her—she's been watching me.

Does it mean—?

Has she been in the same boat as me the entire time, longing for us to reunite?

My thoughts collide, coming too quickly to separate. I breathe harder, then sputter when one glaring possibility crosses my mind.

"So, you've seen the news about me then?" I venture, voice flat and empty.

She scrunches her nose in confusion. "What news? I've been up to my elbows in cookie dough and sugar to meet the holiday rush."

Relief spills through me. She doesn't have the lies those articles have spread about me being a loose canon tainting her view of me. I get to be the one to tell her the truth.

I start skating again and tug her with me. "Well, you remember how I said I was on leave?"

"Yes."

I sigh. "It's not entirely true. My contract was terminated last week."

Her head whips around. "What? Can they do that?"

"Unfortunately, it does happen. And in my case, it was my word against another player's with more value in the eyes of the team's ownership."

Holly pulls a disgusted face. "That's unbelievable. Can't you fight back?"

"If it were a private incident, yeah. But there's been a PR storm since the story broke."

I ruffle the hair on my nape with a sigh, explaining the whole story of how I found Chet and the girl he was harassing, how it led to the fight and the subsequent paparazzi stories setting the situation on fire before I was forced off the team.

"Oh my god," she whispers.

"I'm sorry for not telling you sooner. I just...wasn't ready to face your reaction yet."

She hugs my arm and rests her head on my shoulder. "Don't be. I've known you my whole life. You're not anything like that guy, and you never will be. I'm pissed for you."

"At this point, I want to move on and put Seattle behind me. The other guys on the team are nice enough, but I only stayed with them as long as I did because it took me a long ass time to work my way to the regular roster. I was so focused on helping the team make the playoffs for a chance at the cup, I lost myself and what I wanted."

"So what happens now?" she asks.

"My agent has something lined up for me with a team that's based here."

Even though I only have a little information about this new team that wants me on their roster, my gut tells me it's meant to be. I don't care what their offer is, I'm ready to accept it.

I glide to a stop and hold both Holly's hands in mine. Her eyes bounce back and forth. My heartbeat kicks up a notch, drumming faster with all the pent-up desire I've carried while waiting for this chance to come back to my girl. I lay it all on the table for her.

"If there's a chance for me to stay in New England, I'm taking it. Because this is where I want to be." I pull her closer, her chest brushing mine. "Right here."

CHAPTER 13
HOLLY

LATER THAT NIGHT, I'm brewing mulled wine that smells divine. The spiced, tangy aroma fills the first floor of the cabin. Caleb found a festive record in his parents' collection and jazzy holiday tunes play from the record player while the fire he fed crackles with heat.

I hum along to the song and stir the simmering pot.

"That smells so fucking good." Caleb leans over me from behind.

He's a comforting, solid presence at my back. The urge to lean against him tempts me. He makes a gravelly noise of appreciation that ignites a burst of excitement in my core.

We skated on the pond for a while after he told me he plans to stay in New England. Neither of us said anything about holding hands the entire time.

Something has shifted between us. Something I've been resisting against every time he's been patiently testing my resolve.

The walls I'd erected to protect myself from being vulnerable in front of him have crumbled to dust. I'm teetering on the edge, ready to jump but afraid to fall.

Because I know once I do, I'll have to admit I'm irrevocably, helplessly in love with Caleb. And I have been for years. Breaking up didn't stop it, only buried it.

He plays with my hair, twirling a lock around his finger. "Is it almost ready?"

"Yes. I wish I could use the hot tub. The fireplace is nice to drink by, but a mulled wine under the string lights on the porch and a view of the stars? It's the perfect cozy atmosphere to enjoy this in." I sigh dreamily. "I was looking forward to it as part of my vacation plan when I packed the ingredients."

I brought the cutest bikini, too. I'm bummed I won't get the chance to wear it.

"You've got it," he says.

"Huh?" I turn away from the stove as he opens the door.

"I'll shovel it out for you. It won't take long."

My heart flutters and I think back to what he said when he carried me up the hill after I hurt my ankle. *Anything for you.*

A smile tugs at my lips. I peek out the window to

watch him dig out the hot tub on the porch. He turns on the string lighting to cast the steaming hot tub in a golden swath of light and makes quick work of it.

I change into my bikini and slip on an oversized hoodie—the one I've stolen from him. When I pad downstairs, he's waiting for me.

Caleb's gaze roves over me, lingering on my thick thighs with a darkening gaze. He pushes out a rough exhale and runs a hand through his tousled hair.

"Hot tub's all ready for you," he says.

"Thank you."

I ladle the mulled wine into two glasses, garnishing them with dried orange slices and cinnamon sticks. He accepts the one I hand him and trails after me.

Outside, he watches me intently as if he's reluctant to let me out of his sight. I pause after setting my drink on the edge of the hot tub. Meeting his burning gaze, I peel his hoodie off, showing off the red plaid bikini with frills that flaunts my curves.

Before I have to ask, his hand is there. I take it gratefully and climb in, entering the water with a shivering sigh. The fizzing bubbles burst against my skin and the temperature difference makes the rest of me break out in goosebumps.

Caleb's throat bobs with a swallow. He angles his glass back and forth, tearing his enraptured attention from me to stare into the drink before taking a long sip.

"If you need anything, call for me. I'll leave you to enjoy yourself," he rasps.

The night air combined with the heady mulling spices bolster my impulses. My hand darts out, grasping his wrist to stop him.

"What's wrong?" The glow of the lights draped around the porch catch his eyes, making the green more vivid and alluring.

"Stay with me," I murmur.

The request encompasses everything I want right now. Him joining me in the steamy water to enjoy the mulled wine I made together. Him staying in New England. Him staying with me and never letting go again.

Caleb inclines his head with a hooded gaze. "I didn't bring swim shorts."

"Since when has that been something that stopped you?"

I sink into the water and lift my brows in challenge, sipping my drink. The corner of his mouth lifts in a lopsided, dimpled smirk that steals my breath.

He reaches behind his head and tugs off his sweater. I only have a moment to enjoy the view of the fitted t-shirt he's wearing underneath before he loses that too, revealing his delectable bare chest. Finally, he kicks off his jeans and tosses them in the clothes pile with the hoodie.

It's my turn for my eyes to roam everywhere that I didn't indulge in the first morning here. God, he's so hot.

His chiseled pecs and those irresistible broad shoulders. Muscled arms that engulf me in the best embrace. Sculpted abs I want to lick.

He joins me in the water with a rumble of satisfaction when he lowers himself beside me.

"Nice, right?" I settle against the jets and admire the twinkling stars overhead beyond the pine trees.

"Yeah."

He's not looking at the starry sky. His gaze is locked on me.

Our legs brush together. Exhilaration simmers in my stomach. He's so close my side tingles with awareness.

The humid condensation rising off the water amplifies the hushed yet enticing sense that we're teetering on the precipice of something.

For a while, we're both quiet as we drink our mulled wine. It's nice. I don't feel like I have to talk to fill the space. With him, I can just be.

"Remember that time we came here, just the two of us?" He tilts his head back and peers at me from the corner of his eye. "That was the best summer of my life."

I bite my lip and nod. "Mine too."

A beat of silence passes. He's the one to break it.

"If that's true, why didn't we work out?" He sets his drink aside and shifts closer to me, brows pinching. "We were good together. Weren't we?"

"We were," I agree, distracting myself by tracing the water droplets on his chest.

We drift closer. His arm circles my waist and his fingertips skim up my spine as his stare pins me in place.

"So...?" he prompts gruffly.

"So what?" I murmur ruefully. "We were young, and it was exciting sneaking around with you because you were my best friend's brother."

He shakes his head. "It was more than that."

"I—"

He grasps my chin to make me look at him. His eyes glimmer with a rawness that makes my breath catch. Desire swoops in my stomach. His arm is locked around my waist, not allowing me to escape his searching stare full of longing.

"Tell me the truth. You walked away from us. I've been wondering about it all this time, Holly."

My teeth scrape my lip. He pulls it free and soothes it with his thumb.

"I overheard you on the phone with your coach," I explain. "He was giving you a talk about where your focus needed to be if you wanted to go pro, and you downplayed that we were dating, saying you weren't seeing anyone. All while I was naked in your bed. It broke my heart, so I took it as my sign to get out before I was in too deep with you."

My chest tightens because it was too late, my heart already belonged to him.

"Fuck," he mutters. "My coach had that talk with everyone to weed out the players who aren't serious. It was —you were never supposed to hear that. Is that why you didn't answer any of my messages when I went back to campus?"

"Yes."

"I didn't mean what I said to him. I was serious about both—you and hockey."

I draw a shaking breath, trying to line up what he's saying with how I remember it.

"You didn't chase after me. Not for long, anyway. So I figured I was right that what we had was only a summer fling."

He grabs my shoulders. "I thought you hated me because every time I tried to text or call you, you ignored it."

My gaze falls. "I told myself I did. I was afraid if I answered I would break down from missing you because I...I felt too much for you. But I had my own goals to work on, and you had yours."

A laugh of disbelief puffs out of him. "Do you know how long I've been in—?" He hangs his head. "I've kept my old text conversation with you pinned to the top of my messages."

My stomach bottoms out. "You have?"

"Yeah. I read through it all the time. Sometimes I tell you about my day before deleting it." He swipes a hand over his jaw. "But the things I've really wanted to tell you...those I keep in a note on my phone. It's full of years' worth of messages I've never sent you but desperately wished I could've."

I swallow hard, my heart fluttering uncontrollably. He's really been yearning for me the entire time we've been apart?

"I'm such an idiot for ever letting you go," he says. "I've regretted it every damn day."

"Really?"

"Yeah. Every chance I could, I kept up with what you were up to online. I'd hang on everything Layla said about you. There were so many times I talked myself in and out of showing up at your doorstep, even if you slammed the door in my face because you didn't want to see me again."

I'm shocked. He's a star hockey player who could have any woman he wanted. Yet he's been hung up on me.

As much as I've been stuck on him.

My lips slide together and I offer a confession of my own. "No one's ever measured up to you. I've secretly compared everyone I went on dates with to the guy I couldn't erase from my mind no matter how hard I tried to forget about you. There's hardly a day that passes where I don't think of you."

A hoarse noise escapes him. The air around us thickens with an all-consuming tension.

His arms tighten around me, one palm gliding down to

knead my waist while the other slowly winds the tie of my bikini around his finger. My palms glide up his chest to rest on his shoulders. I wet my lips. His gaze tracks the darting of my tongue.

"What do the unsent messages on your phone say?" I whisper.

"I'll let you read them all later," he promises.

The steam coming off the water swirls around us, creating the hypnotic sense of time slowing. It feels like we're the only two people in the world.

Our drinks sit forgotten at the edge of the hot tub. The scant inches between us disappear with each hazy breath.

Caleb stares into my eyes and tugs on my bikini ties. A gasp escapes me as the material loosens enough to partially expose my breasts.

Desire pulses through me. I don't want to deny it any longer.

"Fuck it," I breathe.

The water sloshes as I crash into him, sealing my lips against his in a kiss that quickly grows wild and desperate. He groans, parting his lips to meet my tongue while pulling the other tie on my suit.

My bikini top falls off, leaving me in only my bottoms. I loop my arms around his neck, moaning at the sensation of my nipples dragging against his wet chest while we make out.

He makes a ragged sound against my mouth, pulling

me further onto his lap. His erection teases between my thighs. I rock against it, kissing him harder.

His palm squeezes my ass and I tear my mouth from his to hang my head back. It's so good, I could come just from this.

"Caleb," I gasp out.

"Say my name again." He sounds absolutely wrecked.

As his lips find a sensitive spot, I moan his name again. He growls in approval, holding me tighter.

Molten heat spills through me, thrumming in the pit of my stomach. I want more.

He's right there with me, lifting me by his firm grip on my ass. I squeal, wrapping my legs around him as water runs off our bodies.

His teeth graze my throat teasingly before he brings his lips to my ears.

"I want you in my bed, sugar."

CHAPTER 14
CALEB

THIS IS everything I've missed and longed for in the last seven years.

I have Holly in my arms. Her perfect mouth is on mine, demanding and needy. Her wet, supple body pressed against me everywhere.

Christ, those heavenly fucking tits of hers will be the death of me. She's got me completely wrecked, already on the edge.

We barely stop kissing once we leave the hot tub. I let her down only so we don't slip and break our necks getting out, then I haul her against me where she belongs and pick her up again.

I forget about drying off, forget about the icy chill whipping around us as I carry her inside, forget about everything else in the world that isn't the woman I finally have in my arms.

My girl.

"Caleb."

Holly moans when I set her on the edge of the kitchen island to take my time devouring her mouth with a searing kiss. The sound of my name on her lips so fucking divine.

"In a minute, baby. I have to kiss you first," I say against her swollen lips.

Her giggle evolves into another whimper of pleasure. "We're getting everything wet. As hot as this is, you know the cabin rules."

"Fuck the cabin rules right now," I scoff. "The only rule I care about is that you come first—always."

She shudders, squeezing my sides with her thighs while I torment the sensitive spot on her neck with a claiming kiss that I hope leaves my mark. I love every sound I'm drawing from her, greedy for more.

I plan to spend all night worshiping every inch of her until I'm thoroughly reacquainted with the love of my life.

She sinks her fingers in my hair while my tongue flicks against her pert nipple. The scrape of her nails against my scalp elicits a strangled cry from me.

My cock is so hard I'm having trouble thinking straight.

All my thoughts converge on one thing: *her*.

I can't decide if I want to spread her out on the

counter and bury my face between her lush thighs to taste her pussy or see how many of my fingers she can take when I fuck her with them first.

I want *everything* with her at once. To take my time. To make her unravel for me hard and fast. To make love to her all night.

My teeth graze her nipples as a fiercely possessive side of me takes over.

Holly is *mine*. Tonight, tomorrow, on Christmas—for all fucking time.

Her body arches. With a sharp gasp, she tugs my head away from her breasts and leans in to kiss my jawline.

"Take me to bed, Caleb," she murmurs against my ear.

Fuck.

Those are five words I've only heard her say in my dreams. Arousal pulses through me, hot and throbbing right to my rigid cock. I've never almost come in my own pants so fast in my life.

"God, I've wanted to hear you say that."

"Then don't keep me waiting." She tilts her head with the sexiest expression, her plush lips curved playfully and her blue eyes radiant with desire.

I know my universal truth then and there—I'll do anything in my power to give her the entire goddamn world.

Right after I fuck her senseless to make up for all the lost time between us.

Holly's arms circle my neck and she hovers her mouth over mine. "I need you inside me."

My grip spasms on her waist. I toss her over my shoulder, enjoying the hell out of the way it makes her squeal with laughter.

"Anything for you, sugar cookie," I croon with a low, smoky chuckle.

Her ass jiggles perfectly when I smack it. Grinning, I hug her legs tighter and give her thigh a teasing bite on our way upstairs.

When we reach my room, I set her down gently and fall to my knees before her. Kissing my way up her thighs, I knead them with reverence. As I reach her apex, I leer up at her.

She catches her lip with her teeth, chest heaving with labored breaths. I hook my fingers in her bikini bottom and peel it off her, discarding it once she steps out of it. Gazing up at her completely bare for me, I swallow hard.

She's perfect.

Absolutely fucking *perfect*.

And I'm a man who's starving for her.

I press my face against her abdomen with a groan before I lose control. Trailing open mouthed kisses across her soft skin, I make my way to her mound and tease her with the tip of my tongue tracing the seam of her folds.

"Oh my god," she hisses when I brush her clit.

She lifts her leg over my shoulder to give me better

access. I grin against her body. That's my greedy girl, not asking for what she wants but demanding it of me. I'm all too happy to oblige.

My mouth covers her pussy, fervent and unrelenting. I keep her balance steady with an arm locked around her leg and slip a finger into her, working it in and out of her until she starts rocking her hips. I give her more, fucking her with my fingers as I suck on her clit.

"Oh, oh f-fuck! Right there. I'm going to come." She grips the back of my head with a hazy cry, keeping me right where she craves me.

I let her have her exactly what she needs, lapping at her clit until she stills with a gasp. The sound she makes when she comes is music to my ears.

Easing back, I drink in the sight of her blissed out from my mouth. I can't wait to make her come while my cock is buried inside her.

Once she catches her breath, she cards her fingers through my hair affectionately and wipes her thumb across my lip coated with her wetness. I kiss it tenderly.

"How was that?" I ask.

"Very fucking good," she answers with a huff of amusement. "But I want to make you feel good, too."

"Yeah?" I rub my face into her palm. "I'll bet it feels real damn nice when I fill you up with my cock."

"Mm, question is...which hole do you want first? Decisions, decisions," she taunts, tapping her lips and licking her finger suggestively.

Holy fucking hell.

I lose my briefs and tackle her to the bed. She giggles as we bounce, capturing my mouth for another kiss that lights my chest up brighter than an entire block decorated for the holidays.

I end up on my back as she turns her attention to my aching erection. But with her ass within reach, I need more. I tug her on top of me until I have her pussy at mouth level, groaning in relief as her lips close around the head of my cock.

"Your mouth feels incredible. Christ, it's better than I remember," I praise.

She hums, taking my shaft deeper until she reaches the base. My eyes roll back in my head and an uncontrollable moan slips out of me. She works my length, making the filthiest slurping noises without shame. I show her my appreciation by devouring her until her pace falters as I bring her pleasure to a peak.

Having my girl sucking on my cock while I eat her pussy? It's heaven. The only thing I know will top this is being inside her.

The sweet torment of her mouth combined with the needy sounds she's making are too much. I'm too close and, as much as I want her to keep sucking my cock until she's swallowing every last drop of my come, I stop her.

"Please. Please, Holly, I need to fuck you. I'm begging you," I breathe hoarsely.

"Holy shit," she whispers as she strokes my thigh.

"What?"

"No one's ever begged me for it before. That's so incredibly hot."

"I'm going to beg for you every damn day," I warn with a dopey ass grin. "I'll never stop needing you this badly. Do you see what you do to me? I'm wild for you, baby."

She eases herself up, giving me the best fucking view of her straddling my face. I can't help myself, I strain my neck and taste her pussy again with a rough grunt of satisfaction. My cock throbs as pleasure courses through my veins, rushing south.

Holly moans, spreading wider for me. I lick and suck her soaked folds until her legs shake and she comes on my face again.

"Now come here and sit pretty on my cock. I want to feel your pussy sinking down and taking every inch," I say gruffly.

When I sit up to get a condom, she stops me. My stare bores into her.

"You don't want me to put on a condom?"

"We don't need anything else between us," she says.

I nod with a heavy-lidded gaze. She braces over me for a kiss as she settles on top of me. It goes from tender to sizzling with passion within moments. I knead her ass and grind the tip of my cock through her slick folds.

Our bodies move together in sync, writhing until I hold her still and press inside. We both moan in unison.

The instant I first experience her wet, glorious heat almost sends me right over the edge.

I hold her close and roll her to her back. My mouth falls open as my cock thrusts deeper and my gaze roves her beautiful face.

She's a vision with her pink tendrils of hair fanned across the bed, cheeks flushed, and her eyes locked on mine.

My chest swells until it feels like it's going to burst open. My composure threatens to break.

I'm teetering as I draw back and thrust with a rough exhale. Her eyes fall shut with a pleased sigh and she winds her arms around my shoulders to hold me closer.

"Wait, wait," I rasp.

The urgent words tumble out with a trembling, raw whimper I can't smother. Fuck, I've waited for this. *Her.*

I clutch her hips in desperation. Stopping might end me, but I need a minute or I'm going to lose it.

"Give me a second or this will be over too quickly. I want to savor you."

Holly shivers. "I'm not going anywhere."

"It's...been a while." I nuzzle into her throat, mouthing at her pulse point until she arches for me. I groan into her soft skin, needing everything at once. "Fuck, I want you so badly. I've been waiting so long for this. Seven years with only my hand and you in my head, baby."

"What?"

Her fingers thread into my hair and she uses her grip to make me meet her stunned gaze. I can't help the aroused noise it pulls from me.

My grin spreads slowly in satisfaction for catching her off guard. Did she really think I wanted anyone but her?

"What's that look for, baby?"

"You're serious? You haven't... Not with anyone else?" A wrinkle forms between her brows that I want to smooth with my thumb.

"Not once."

"Why?" Her searching gaze bounces between mine.

"None of them were you. It was always you."

"Caleb," she whispers shakily.

"Don't believe me yet? That's okay. Let me show you." My lips brush hers. "I'll spend all night proving to you that you're it for me."

I kiss her hard as I thrust my cock deep inside her. She wraps her legs around my hips, writhing beneath me from the pace I set.

"I'm yours," I say against her jaw between kisses. "All fucking yours, baby."

She clings to me with a hitched cry. Hooking an arm under her knee, I lift her leg and adjust my angle to find the spot that used to make her scream. I grin when her body flutters around me with her heightened ecstasy.

"There it is. Feel that? How your pussy's squeezing my cock?"

"Please," she hisses.

"Please what, Holly? Use your words. Tell me what you need," I rasp.

"Don't stop. Make me come," she demands.

I fuck her harder and pet her clit, grinning when she gets loud. It's a shame there isn't anyone around the cabin for miles to hear how gorgeous she sounds. I want the entire world to know she's mine.

My hips falter as I skate too close to the brink of my building orgasm. I can't hold on much longer. I pour all my focus into her.

She whimpers as she crests the cliff and tips over the edge. I'm right there with her.

As it hits me, I bury my cock in her, shuddering from coming so hard I almost blackout.

We collapse in a tangle of limbs, catching our breath. I'm mindful not to crush her, rolling to my side and tucking her against me.

The piece I've missed since she walked away slots back into place, making me whole, no longer hollowed out from longing for my girl.

Holly traces random patterns on my chest with her

nails, pretty features set in wonder. I hook a finger under her chin, tilting it up for a kiss.

A profound sense of peace spreads through me, along with drowsiness. I lazily skim my palm down her spine to grip her ass. My fingers slip between her legs to play with her pussy, feeling my come beginning to leak from her.

"What's that smirk for?" she asks.

"I'm picturing how you look with my come dripping out of your pussy," I answer smugly. "I want to admire it, but I need to rest for a second before I can move."

She smacks my chest with a snort. "Okay, you cocky caveman perv."

I capture her hand and hold it against my skin, caressing it. "Only for you."

With a teasing growl, I roll on top of her and kiss her senseless.

CHAPTER 15
HOLLY

THE ONLY THING that makes life better when you're snowed in alone with your best friend's brother is falling in love with him again and having him bang your brains out all over the family cabin.

The unlimited orgasms? Mind-blowing. But the next time I visit the cabin with Layla or the rest of his family, I won't be able to look any of them in the eye.

"Have more water," Caleb insists.

"If I drink anymore, I'll have to pee, like, ten times in the next hour," I reply with a huff.

"You need to hydrate. It's important," he scolds, plopping the water bottle back in my hands.

"Fine."

The attitude is just for show.

In reality, a tingling, happy thrill shoots through me in

response to his caretaking. After our first round in bed, he carried me to the shower and washed me with dedicated gentleness. Then he devoted himself to making me fall apart all over again. He hasn't stopped since.

"What?" I ask him when I down half the water, quenching the thirst I'd been ignoring as I caught up on my emails.

He braces his hands on the back of the couch where I'm laying and stares at my mouth. "I want to kiss you."

I giggle, taking another sip of water. "So kiss me."

He grunts. "If I do, I won't be able to stop myself. I'm not trying to wear you out."

"Who's complaining?"

I trap my tongue between my teeth with a wicked smile, drawing my bare leg up to peek from the blanket. The only thing I have on is his old Heston U college hoodie, and not another scrap of clothing.

I really need to finish answering my emails, but...he's too tempting. I haven't gone more than five minutes without wanting him since we kissed in the hot tub, not counting all the years he secretly stayed tethered to my heart.

"You know I'm ready for you under here. All I have on is your hoodie. No panties. Wet and waiting for you to slip it in," I croon with a coy tilt of my head.

I have no idea where this confident vixen has sprung from, but I like it. I've always felt assured in my sexuality, yet I've never been this bold. He's inspired a side of myself I never knew.

"Fucking hell," he grumbles into his hands as he scrubs his face. "You're going to be the death of me, woman."

"And what a sweet, oh-so-delicious way to go," I agree with a blissful sigh. "Okay, you're right. We need a breather. I have to get this work done. Leo and Hazel don't know how to answer them without asking me questions. They're piling up, so it's easier for everyone if I do it myself."

"Deal." He sprawls on one of the armchairs by the fireplace and studies me with a crooked smile that makes my heart skip a beat.

I bite my lip, glancing at the date on my phone. Five more days until Christmas. Last night when we finally came up for air after being wrapped up in each other, we found out road crews were beginning to clear the residential roads on the mountain.

"Do you think they're going to get to our section of roads before Christmas? Or do you think we'll be stuck here still?" I ask.

"It depends on which side they started with and how much the roads have iced over. But if we are, we can call your family and mine on Christmas Day on FaceTime so you can still see them," he suggests.

I nod. "I can't believe we might miss out. I've never been away from my family for Christmas. Even when I moved to Mayfield permanently after college, I've always gone home to spend it with them."

"It was weird for me the first year I wasn't home for the holidays. Since the regular season is a tight schedule, we only get a short break. I don't always go back."

I play with the dainty bows on the ends of my loose French braids. "I'm going to miss out on decorating with everyone. It's one of our favorite family traditions. I could bake us a Christmas tree cake, I suppose, but it won't be the same."

He strokes his jaw with a twinkle in his eye. "You want a tree? I'll get you a tree."

I sit up. "You will?"

"Of course." He pushes to his feet and stops by me to drop a kiss on the top of my head. "Wait here. I'll be back with it in a bit."

I twist around, gaping at him as he puts on his boots and coat. "Like, you're going to go chop one down for me? A real tree?"

He winks. "Sure am. We'll make our own holiday traditions."

My heartbeat thuds hard. I lay a hand over it as he exits the cabin. An elated bout of laughter flies out of me.

I'm so excited, I feel like jumping around. I've never had a real tree before. My family uses a perfectly usable hand me down, but I've always wanted to decorate a real one. I never asked because I don't like making a burden of myself.

Guilt pangs in my stomach when I get off the coach. I need to finish my emails, but I want to dig through all the stuff I overpacked to collect as many of my hair bows as possible to fill the tree. Leo's managing things the best he can with Hazel and Leta's extra help, but he's still not me. He won't be able to handle everything the way I do.

I'll take a quick break, then I'll get back to it.

As I'm collecting whatever I find around the cabin to go with my massive collection of bows, I finally check the text I missed from Layla. She messaged me early this morning while I was...otherwise occupied by her brother when he found the vibrator I stashed in one of my bags. He didn't stop playing with me until I lost count of how many times I came and had turned into a quivering mess.

I really want to tell her what happened with Caleb because we tell each other everything. Except, I kept it a secret from her before when I first fell for her brother.

We're older now. Sneaking around feels silly.

I stare at her text as uncertainty holds me back. I won't tell her without talking to Caleb about it first.

LAYLA

Have you made it through the movies we have stashed there?

HOLLY

Yup. We made a drinking game out of it.

LAYLA

Omg, I'm jealous. I want to play. Let's go back to the cabin for New Year's Eve instead of going out.

HOLLY

That might be too soon for me. We'll see if I escape by then [laughing emoji]

LAYLA

Think about it! Bonus, we'll save so much money. I need to scrounge every penny for my move to Mayfield [thinking emoji] Ok, but downside…no hot men to kiss at midnight and dick us down after.

HOLLY

Or girls [heart emoji] [rainbow emoji]

LAYLA

Yes. You know what? Probably better. Think we can convince Hana to join us? It's been forever since the three of us got to hang together.

HOLLY

This definitely is the solid start to our New Year's plan.

LAYLA

Just me and my bestie girls! We don't need anyone but each other.

My lips twist wryly at the long string of heart emojis she sends me. I send her just as many back.

I adore her. While I share her sentiment, there is someone else I need.

By the time I've gathered all my potential decorations in a pile on the coffee table, changed into a cute satin disco ball sleep set with my embroidered bow slippers, and powered through the rest of my emails, Caleb returns.

I beam, holding the door open for him as he hoists the tree he chopped down for me onto the porch. "Oh my god, it's beautiful!"

"Picked the best one for you." He shoots me a heart-stopping dimpled smile.

"I love it!"

He props it against the house, shaking off the excess snow from the branches. Once he's satisfied, he grabs a tree stand from the shed and makes space in the sitting room inside.

"How's here by the window?" he asks.

"Perfect."

He gets everything set up while I supervise. I'm barely able to contain my amazement. We haven't done anything to the tree yet and it already looks fantastic.

I inhale deeply, eyelashes fluttering. "It smells so nice."

"My grandma's always had the same thought. Grandpa always went out without fail when we spent our holidays here and brought her back the biggest, prettiest trees he could find," he says.

I select a thin white ribbon with a scalloped lace edge and tie a bow on one of the branches. I light up, adding another until the middle section is dotted with the bows I usually use to tie up my hair. When I reach for the next one, I find him watching me with a tender expression.

"Will you help me decorate?" I tie a bow and offer it to him.

He accepts it, leaning in to brush a kiss against my lips. "Tell me where you want it."

"Up high where I can't reach." I point to an ideal sprig.

The corner of his mouth quirks. Grasping my waist, he boosts me up in a smooth show of strength and perches me on his shoulder.

"Show off." I fight a smile.

His thumb strokes my thigh. "For you? Always. Find a good spot for that bow."

We get the top of the tree filled in with ribbons and the other odds and ends I collected from around the house, including wooden napkin holders with winter motifs, a set of woodland creatures made from pinecones, extra dried orange slices I brought for my mulled wine recipe, and some of my two-toned baking twine. To top it off, I add my biggest bow hair clip as the topper.

Once the upper half of the tree is complete, he sets me down. We work on the bottom section together. I set a snow globe on the mantel next to the tree as the finishing touch.

"Where'd you find that?"

I trace the carved trees on the base. "On top of a cabinet in the kitchen while I was raiding it for the napkin rings."

The rustic cabin inside the glass is a close match for the one we're in.

"It feels like we're inside the snow globe right now," I murmur. "Our private bubble away from the world."

His hand rests at the small of my back. "The tree looks great."

"It does," I agree warmly. "Thank you for doing this."

"Of course." He curls his fingers around my hip and kisses my temple.

"I used to love looking at this when I was here in the winter." I gesture to the snow globe.

"Yeah?"

I nod. "I love snow globes. When I was little, I collected them. I even wished I could be inside one."

"Did you think they were pretty and made of magic?"

"Yes, but also because this is what my head has always felt like."

He hums inquisitively, waiting patiently for me to explain myself. I shake it so the snow flies everywhere and show him.

"All the snow swirling around me is the chaos I exist in

and I'm the only one who knows how to handle it all. When it's storming, it's a lot to manage. But there's peace in there too when I've weathered the storm."

"Alone?" he clarifies with a frown. "You're putting a lot of pressure on yourself."

I shrug. "I thrive under pressure."

"But you don't have to without someone else to help you ease it. I don't want you to be in your head alone," he says softly. "I want to be in the snow globe with you, sugar."

A lump forms in my throat at him wanting to be my support, making it difficult to speak. I melt against him, tucking my head beneath his chin. He holds me tight in his embrace.

A million worries constantly flit through my head.

Yet none of them matter to me right now. Caleb's presence chases everything away until it's just the two of us together.

CHAPTER 16
HOLLY

"How CAN you pick apple cobbler over bourbon bread pudding?" I plant my hands on the island counter across from Caleb. "Oh, I don't think so. I'm going to prove you wrong right now."

He shrugs. "I've always been an apple cobbler guy. Is that wrong?"

"No." I lean in to level him with a grave look. "But it's not right, either. My bourbon maple pecan bread pudding is the best in New England. As soon as you try it, you'll change your mind."

It's the middle of the day. After he made breakfast—something I'm growing accustomed to, allowing myself the simple enjoyment of being looked after without having to worry about one more thing like what I'll make to eat—I got the belated approval back for a New Year's party custom cookie order.

If I test the designs today I can email a detailed step by step guide to Leo for him, Hazel, and Leta to at least get the base cookies done by the time I'm back at the bakery to manage the decorating stage.

That is, until Caleb challenged my beloved bourbon bread pudding, my favorite holiday treat. The cookie test run will have to wait until I make him reconsider this.

He circles the island and catches my wrist as I reach for one of my aprons.

"You don't like the idea of not being right," he muses.

My chin lifts. "Hate it. I'm right and I'm going to make you eat your words. Right after you eat my pie."

He tugs me into him, his breath ghosting over my ear. "How about I have you instead? You're my real favorite meal, morning and night."

I fight off a blush. "Nice try at distracting me. You just don't want me to make you the best damn winter dessert you'll ever taste."

"Easy. That's you."

He kisses the sensitive spot beneath my ear, smiling against my throat when my resolve to work evaporates and I sag against him. My teeth drag over my lip as his fingertips skim beneath my sweater to trace my skin.

"Put your apron on," he rasps, pausing a beat before adding, "Just your apron."

My stomach dips with arousal. I hold my arms overhead to help him peel my top off. His rumble of approval reverberates from his chest against my back. He takes his time caressing my bare skin, leaning over my shoulder to watch as he pulls the cups of my bra down to expose my breasts.

My eyes fall shut and my breathing quickens when he circles my nipples with a light caress.

"Caleb," I whimper. "Please."

"Please what, baby?" He sounds so relaxed and nonchalant compared to the blaze of desire he's igniting within me.

"More." I push my tits into his hands.

"My greedy girl."

He chuckles, gratifying me with a firmer touch. His hands cup my tits and he rolls my nipples with his thumbs until they're aching in time with the sensual pulse of my desire.

I audibly mourn the loss when he lets go to unclasp the bra and work my leggings off. I'm not wearing any underwear. He spares a kiss for my ass cheek before he pulls me back against his chest, completely bare. The stiff ridge of his cock in his pants teases me when it brushes me.

"Look at you," he whispers in awe.

Caleb gets one of my brightly colored aprons off the hook and puts it on me. A delicious thrill runs through me at being nude beneath it, barely covered by the cute patterned fabric.

Winding the ties around his hands, he pulls the material taut against my front and makes a rough noise by my ear.

"I've been thinking about this nonstop," he rasps.

"Have you?" I reply tartly.

"It's those fucking bows you always wear. Makes me want you like…"

His fingers curl gently around my wrists and he guides them into place folded behind my back before loosely wrapping my apron ties around them.

"Is this okay?"

Molten heat spills through me.

I tip my head back to peer at him through my lashes. "Do I seem bothered by the idea of you tying me up?"

"Yes or no, sugar. Use your words." He nips my shoulder, then kisses it.

"Yes," I answer cheekily.

He rewards me by capturing my lips with an openmouthed kiss that makes my knees weak. His strong arm holds me up.

"See how sexy consent is?" Caleb murmurs.

I can't help swaying. He makes me feel out of control when I'm with him in the best way possible. Normally I cling to control with a vice grip, yet with him I can let go knowing he's got me.

"Well? Tie me up with a pretty bow and fuck me already," I sass with a teasing rotation of my ass against his erection.

"Keep running that mouth, baby. You know how much I like it when you give me that bossy attitude," he says against my ear as he cinches the ties to secure my arms.

A shiver races down my spine. My nipples are stiff, dragging against the material of the apron when I arch my back seeking more of his touch.

He caresses my sides, pushing beneath the apron to splay his hand over my soft abdomen while kissing a path up my throat. I sigh at the first brush of his fingers on my clit, rocking my hips with each stroke. I strain with the need to touch him back, turned on even more when I can't because my hands are bound behind my back.

He stops playing with my pussy just as the building heat in my core is close to exploding. I protest, only to choke it back when he encourages me to bend over the counter. A smoky rumble sounds from him, making my toes curl.

I'm tied up and spread on display for him in the filthiest sense.

"Do you like me like this?"

"You look like a tasty fucking treat," he says, hushed and reverent.

His praise lights me up from within, sending a wave of satisfying tingles across my skin.

"You're so damn beautiful. I'm going to enjoy eating you up until you're a gorgeous fucking mess for me," he promises, voice dripping with sinful intent.

A gasp tears from me when he kneels and spreads me further. I squirm from the invisible weight of his gaze. He leans in, ghosting his hot breath over my pussy. My breath hitches when, at last, he flicks his tongue out to taste me with a deep, passionate hum.

He abandons the teasing licks in favor of burying his face against the back of my thighs with a ragged whimper and devouring me.

It's as if he can't get enough of me. My back arches and my fingers flex, grasping at nothing from the confines of my apron ties.

Caleb knows exactly how to take me apart at the seams with his talented mouth. Although I'm the one at his mercy, bound and spread for him, there's something heady and powerful about having him on his knees groaning like he's in heaven giving me pleasure.

I'm close to the edge when he pauses. Fabric rustles, followed by a click and an audible buzzing sound. He presses a smooth fluttering silicone object against me—my vibrator.

A louder moan flies out of me. My body spasms, both in shock and heightened pleasure from the toy being sprung on me unsuspectedly.

"H-have you just been carrying that around in your

pocket this whole time today?" I push out breathlessly, fighting to speak through the mind-melting ecstasy.

A smirk is evident in his voice when he responds, "Yup. I was planning to make out with you and surprise you with it. This is better."

He sounds so casual, like he's reading hockey stats rather than using a vibrator on me while I'm tied up by my own apron strings and bent over the counter for him to play with. Before I can respond, my body erupts in a throbbing current of orgasmic bliss.

"Oh! Oh god!"

He praises me through it. "There you go, sugar. Does that feel nice on your clit? Give me another one. Make that pussy a mess for me."

The orgasm feels endless from his devoted attention and his dirty talk. It stretches into another before the first one fades. My hips buck with a gasp against his face and the toy.

"So good for me," he murmurs against my sensitive skin.

His tongue glides through my folds and delves into my hole as he works my clit with the vibrator.

My mind whites out. All I know is the delirious euphoria of his mouth, the toy, and his encouraging murmurs tipping me over the edge again and again until my body is a twitching, trembling wreck.

When I've lost track of how many orgasms I've shuddered through, he sets the toy aside and stands.

Caleb kisses my spine. "Are you doing okay? Do you want a break, or are you ready for more?"

I writhe, not caring how desperate I sound. "Don't you dare fucking stop yet."

He chuckles warmly. "Can I fuck you like this?"

"Yes," I plead. "I need you inside me so badly."

He covers my body with his and kisses my temple. "You want my cock, baby?"

"Yes, damn it. Fuck me. *Use* me."

He stifles a gruff noise. "So worked up. Me too, sugar. You feel how hard you make me?"

His erection grinds against me. I'm frustrated by the barrier of clothes, wanting to feel the silken heat of his cock completely.

"I'm going to fuck you hard and fast right here on the counter until your pussy is so full of my come I get to admire it dripping out of you after," he croons.

I moan, nodding fervently at the image he paints. "Caleb, please."

"Asking for it so nicely," he teases.

Shoving his pants down, he glides the tip of his cock against me before he lines up. We both cry out in relief when he sinks inside inch by inch until his hips brush mine. I feel so impossibly full with him all the way in, eyes fluttering shut.

"Fuck, you're so wet," he groans.

His hips snap, working into a pace that sets my nerve endings ablaze. The smack of skin on skin is wickedly filthy.

His grip flexes on my hips every time my inner walls clamp on him with growing need. Gritting out a curse, he adjusts his angle until I scream.

"Right there?" I can hear his grin.

It's so good, all I can manage is a nod, pushing back against him with each thrust. Electric sparks flash through me as his cock slams into my pussy.

Unable to do more than lay there and press on my tiptoes, my mind becomes a haze of pleasure unlike any I've ever known.

It makes a white hot coil tighten in my core, the pulsing pressure alluring and inescapable. My body thrums.

Caleb grabs my tied wrists, holding them as he fucks me harder.

A strangled gasp catches in my throat. I can't hold on any longer.

I arch, coming hard. My intense release rushes over me, leaving me boneless, floating in the aftermath.

His thrusts speed up, then stutter as his cock buries deep in me. It throbs as his come spills inside me.

Bracing a hand on the counter, he exhales raggedly. "Jesus."

"Agreed," I slur with a giggle.

He rubs my back tenderly. "Are you okay?"

"More than." I feel like a puddle, enjoying the cool counter beneath my flushed cheek.

"I wasn't too rough?"

"Nope." I sigh blissfully, squeezing his length with my inner walls.

He chokes, resting his forehead against me for a moment. When he pulls out gently, I crane my neck to find him gazing at me like I'm the most beautiful sight in the world.

I shake my ass to make it jiggle, grinning at the fire it ignites in his eyes.

"Careful, sugar. You keep wiggling that dripping pussy and perfect fucking ass at me like that and I'm going to have to fuck you again."

"Oh no," I drawl in a saucy tone that belies the opposite of my words. "Anything but that."

He chuckles, kneading my hips and spreading my cheeks for one last look at the debauched mess he's made of me before his demeanor shifts to his doting caretaker side.

"Hold on for me."

Caleb is careful undoing the apron strings. He helps me up and massages my wrists. I close my eyes, enjoying his big, strong hands rubbing my arms. When he's done, he kisses my fingertips, then gets me a glass of water. He's not satisfied until he makes sure I drink all of it.

He cleans me up first, wetting a washcloth and softly stroking my skin with unwavering focus that leaves me glowing from within. Once he finishes, he bundles me in his arms.

Smiling, he brushes my forehead with his lips. "Don't lift a finger because I'm going to clean the kitchen after I take care of you."

I tuck my face against his chest, hugging him. He carries me to the couch, setting me on his lap.

The fire crackles in the background, keeping the cabin cozy and warm. He wraps a blanket around us and pulls me closer. Our tree completes the perfect ambiance.

When his attention falls to my mouth and he leans in, I meet him first in a languid, heartfelt kiss. He cups my cheek, thumb grazing back and forth. A content sigh leaves him and I echo it, in no hurry to end the kiss.

Eventually we part. His handsome features are serene as he tucks my hair behind my ear.

I'm caught in his adoring gaze. Neither of us feel the need to speak.

We simply exist together. It's the most at peace I've ever felt.

An incandescent happiness fills me. I never knew I could experience such an immense sense of joy.

I thought all I wanted in my life was to open my

bakery. My business does fulfill me, but maybe I still need more. As I picture him at my shop, warmth spreads through me. Maybe all this time I needed to find my way back to him—the one person to completely own my heart.

The work I meant to get ahead on slips to the back of my mind, no longer as urgent to me when I accept that everything will be fine. I don't have to break myself doing everything at once when I'm on a much-needed vacation extended by our circumstances.

Not when I can spend my time enjoying moments like this without rushing to the next thing.

CHAPTER 17
HOLLY

W<small>E DON'T HAVE</small> to spend Christmas at the cabin, after all. The following morning, we get the all clear from the road crew that plowed our exit.

The abrupt change from my bubble disorients me slightly.

We can finally return to reality, and I'm not sure how that may alter things between us.

Do Caleb and I work together once we leave our snow globe tucked away from the world?

I want to believe we can after all we've shared here. My heart is completely his, more entangled than the first time we fell for each other. It will crush me far worse if he breaks it again.

I swallow the sharp pain irritating my throat as I finish

packing. Shaking my head at myself, I cram my slippers into my suitcase.

"Why did I overpack so much for a weekend trip?" I mumble.

The extra stuff I brought came in handy for the length the trip ended up being, but I regret my choices now that I have to fit it all back into my bags.

Caleb appears in the doorway and knocks on the frame. He has my hair ribbons and bow clips in a bag.

"Here, I got all the decorations off the tree."

I hug the bag, fighting the swirl of melancholy. Sure, I have my freedom in time for Christmas. Except it ruins my mood to think of the tree he picked out and chopped down for me won't make it through the holidays. The memory of decorating it with him causes a longing pang in my chest.

He lifts my chin with a crooked finger, eyes flickering between mine. Without another word, he kisses me. I drop the bag of ribbons to wrap my arms around his neck.

"There. That's better. Now you're smiling again," he says.

My cheeks grow hot. I didn't say anything, but he read me easily anyway. A laugh puffs out of me and I duck my face, twirling a lock of hair from my ponytail around my finger.

"Are the cars dug out from the snow?"

"Yeah. I'll take your bags down for you. Leave them to

me." He catches me around the waist before I take more than a step and inclines his head with a pointed look. "I mean it. Don't let me catch you trying to cart them downstairs by yourself."

I fight off a smile and fail to hold it back. "Okay, okay. They're all yours. Thank you."

"Good." He winks, stealing one more kiss before he leaves the room we've shared every night since we kissed in the hot tub.

I fluff the bedding I washed again, running my hands over his pillow. When I hug it and tuck my face into it, I still faintly smell his woodsy aftershave. Flopping onto the bed with a sigh, I close my eyes.

Going home means returning to my bed alone. I'll miss sleeping next to his comforting presence.

It's amazing how quickly I grew accustomed to being wrapped in his arms at night.

I stay like that for several minutes, imagining my head is resting on his chest listening to his steady heartbeat.

When I'm finished packing and can't hold it off any longer, I wheel my bags to the top of the stairs to make it easier for Caleb to grab them. After a quick check in the kitchen to make sure I got all of my baking ingredients and supplies, I head out to the porch for one last look at the breathtaking view.

It truly is a winter wonderland when it snows here.

Vermont is beautiful year round, but there's something so magical about New England in the cold months.

As I'm capturing a few more photos to savor the stunning landscape from the back of the cabin, I hear the familiar honk of a goose call.

"Greta?" I lean over the railing and find her beak rustling through the bushes below.

She clucks in response, fluffy tail feathers wagging. I smile and pop inside to grab the last of the cranberries for her. She eyes me with a sideways look, then waddles over for me to bid her goodbye.

We might have been at odds, but I feel a sense of kindred spirit with her attitude.

"So, are we cool, Greta?"

I toss her some berries and crouch down to take photos of how cute it is when she gobbles them. I can see why Caleb adores her when she coos and comes closer to ask for more. Smiling, I offer her a handful, mimicking the way I watched him feed her when she was sheltered in the shed.

"You're not so bad," I decide.

She honks happily, flapping her wings. I stroke her chest with the back of my fingers.

"There you are," Caleb says from the porch. "My girls are finally getting along."

I shoot him a wry look. "We've reached an agreement. We're willing to share you."

He laughs, bracing his hands on the railing. Greta calls to him, staying by my side to enjoy more cranberries.

"I'm going to lock up." He nods to the cabin.

"Okay. I'm just saying bye to Greta before we go."

When I no longer have food to bribe her with, she ruffles her feathers. I expect her to give me the cold shoulder again and go off to forage for more treats. She hangs around, though. I take a photo with her when she's near me and send it to my siblings.

HAZEL

Aww, she's so cute! I want to hug her!

HOLLY

We had beef, but now we're cool. Tell me why I kind of want to get a goose now?

LEO

Don't geese have teeth? Creepy.

HAZEL

Shut up, Leonard.

LEO

Not my name... [eye roll emoji]

HOLLY

I don't think geese have teeth. Anyway, we're about to leave the cabin. I should be back in Mayfield by this afternoon.

HAZEL

> Finally! I was worried I'd have to make your famous butter tarts and it wouldn't turn out as good.

HOLLY

> Don't say that, yours tastes just as good! Hopefully I'll still have time to make them before we all drive back to Candlewood for Christmas.

LEO

> What time exactly do you think you'll be back? I have a paper I need to send to my professor. I've been too tired to finish it by the time we close the bakery.

Blowing out a breath, I tap out a reply that when I hit city limits, I'd let him know. I want to scold my little brother for mismanaging his time, but I can't. They've both been covering the shop for me while I've been stuck here.

Stress creeps in at the edges of my mind. There are so many things I need to do when I get home, including making sure Leo's grades aren't slipping by having to work overtime for me and baking my annual dessert contribution to our family Christmas dinner.

Sighing, I pet Greta one last time. "You have it so much easier than me. I wish I could wander through a charming woodland looking for tasty berries."

The goose nibbles at the hem of my coat, mistaking the

floral pattern for a treat. Chuckling, I head to the driveway.

I stop in my tracks when I come around to the front of the cabin. My car is warming up for me and it's pulled out of the spot I parked in, turned out for an easy exit. I won't have to make a million point turn to maneuver it because it's already seen to.

Caleb finishes locking up the cabin and storing the key in the security box. He catches me standing there in stunned silence and smiles.

"You're all set. I took care of your car for you. Also checked everything over to make sure it's safe for you to drive. Your oil was a little low, so I topped it off."

An overwhelming rush of emotions swell in my chest —gratitude, surprise, affection.

I turn away with a breathless laugh, blinking away the wetness clinging to my lashes. This is unbelievable. I can't believe I'm going to cry over all the little things he does for me. They're such simple gestures, yet they touch me.

He's the only person who always thinks of me first.

God, I love him. How have I gone so long without him in my life?

"Holly?" He spins me back to him, concern crossing his face.

"Sorry, the wind got in my eye." It's a better excuse than admitting to him I'm getting emotional because he got my car ready for me.

"Let me look." He cradles my face, tilting it with rapt concentration. "Ah, I see the problem."

He kisses me. I melt against him with a smile. His laid-back charisma makes me feel lighter.

Brushing my fringe out of my face when we part, he sighs ruefully. "I know we have to get out of here, but letting you out of my sight is the last thing I want to do."

I nudge him. "You have to. You have a longer drive than I do to get to the city."

He's heading down to New York for a meeting tomorrow with his agent and the new hockey franchise establishing itself in New England.

"I know. Still..." He rests his forehead against mine. "This hasn't been nearly enough time to make up for how long I've missed you."

"Go," I urge with a pleased laugh. "Good luck at your meeting. Will you tell me how it goes?"

He grins. "I've got a good feeling about it from what Trevon's told me. No matter what, it keeps me here. I'm definitely taking the offer, so if you let me take you out to dinner when I'm back from New York I'll tell you all about it."

"Dinner?"

"A date," he clarifies with a hopeful expression that pierces my heart.

I tilt my head. "Caleb Adler, are you asking me out?"

"Are you saying yes?"

I pretend to think about it. His arms lock around me and he swings me around. I squeal, dropping my head back.

"I'm not stopping until you give me an answer." He holds me tighter.

"Yes, I'll go on a date with you."

Slowing our spin, he lowers my feet to the ground with a charming smile that makes me swoon.

"I can't wait to take you out to dinner," he murmurs. "I have something else important I want to tell you."

I bite my lip at the reverence in his tone. He slips his hand in mine and walks me to my car, opening the door for me. I climb in and roll the window down, reluctant to say goodbye to him. He leans in to give me one last kiss.

"Drive safe and let me know when you get in, okay?"

"Thanks, I will. Text me when you make it to the city?"

He nods. "I'll see you soon."

For a moment, I have the urge to blurt that I love him.

The words creep up my throat, dancing to the tip of my tongue. Before I decide if I should or not, he pats the hood of my car and steps back to let me go first.

I wave and pull out, watching him in the rear view mirror. The wind messes up his thick brown hair as he tucks his hands in his pockets and watches me until I'm gone.

The moment I'm on the road, I already miss him.

CHAPTER 18
CALEB

EVERY MINUTE since I've left my family's cabin yesterday, I've counted down the seconds until I see Holly again. The fear that she could still slip through my fingers again haunted my sleep last night. I chase it away with the mantra that she said yes when I asked her out.

I don't want her to believe she's a fling to me. She's my world, and I'm done living without her in my life.

This time I'm doing it all right. I'm going to be clear with her that I'm serious about us. I don't want to keep her a secret and sneak around this time.

I almost call Layla on my way over to Trevon's office in midtown Manhattan. The urge to tell her I'm in love with Holly burns in my chest, but first I want to make sure Holly wants this as much as I do.

Christ, it'll eviscerate me if she turns me down when I

tell her I love her tonight. I'm more nervous for our date than I am for this meeting.

As the private car Trevon sent to the hotel for me pulls up in front of his building, I check my phone.

Seeing a new text with Holly's name makes my heart do a shamelessly excited flip. Not sure how long it'll take for me to get used to seeing messages from her after all the time I spent wishing for her to respond to me.

"Thanks. Have a good day," I tell the driver.

He nods politely. Climbing out, I open her text to read it.

HOLLY

I hope everything goes amazing! [heart emoji]

CALEB

Thanks. Can't wait to see you tonight and tell you all about it. [heart emoji]

HOLLY

Good things always happen for me when I bake this, so I got up early this morning to make it for you. Ignore what it says, I always write the same thing because it's this specific version that has the magic effect. I'm superstitious like that, but I hear you hockey players understand superstitions.

She sends a photo of a small heart-shaped cake with elaborate frosting. The glazed, neat script on it reads *you've got this, you magnificent bitch.* I grin like an idiot, thrilled beyond belief.

"Oh, shit, no way."

A kid walking by with a family decked out in I-heart-New-York tourist memorabilia stops in his tracks. He tugs on the sleeve of the older teen next to him as I'm typing out my thanks to my girl.

"What?" the teen grumbles.

"Look. That's Caleb Adler," the kid hisses.

"Is not." The teen squints at me. "Shit, it is!"

I plaster on the professional persona I slip into when I engage with fans, bracing for this to go south if they've read the articles online from the last couple of weeks. To my relief, they're both genuine when they approach me and ask for my autograph in awestruck stammers.

"No problem." I accept the pen they offer and scrawl my signature across their t-shirts. "You guys big hockey fans?"

"Hell yeah," the older one says. "You're our favorite player."

Something warm and gratifying ping-pongs around my chest. I wasn't sure I'd hear any fan say that about me again.

"I liked you first," his younger brother insists. "When you played for Chicago. But I followed you after you were traded. You're so cool! None of my friends are going to believe I met you."

A huff of laughter escapes me. "Yeah? Thank you."

Their parents snap photos of us together. I wave goodbye and head inside feeling lighter and more energized.

Trevon meets me at the elevator bank once I'm through security. His braided locs are pulled back in a loose tie, and the silver rings on his fingers catch the light as he smooths them down the front of his crisp tailored suit. We clasp hands and he pulls me in to pat my back.

"That mountain air must be a hell of a thing. You look much less like death warmed over," he says.

I smirk. "Something like that. I'm feeling good."

"That's what I like to hear."

We take the elevators to his agency's floor. One of his assistants catches us on our way by the front desk.

"Mr. Hill, the guests you were waiting on for your next meeting have arrived. They're in the conference room."

He nods in thanks. I stop Trevon in the hall before we enter.

"Anything else you want to fill me in on about who we're meeting with? All you've told me is it's a retired player from your time in the league involved and that they're setting up here."

"I've got your back. I wouldn't be so optimistic about

this if I didn't think it was the right call for you," he says. "You trust me?"

My shoulders relax. "Of course. You've never steered me wrong."

"Then let me work, man. Come on." With one of his wide winning smiles, he pushes the door open.

"Hilly," a tall bear of a man with a stubbled jaw looking out the window greets energetically.

"Jonesy," Trevon responds like he's back in the locker room before a game.

My spine straightens. Micah Jones is one of the top hockey players to grace the ice in the last fifteen years. He's around Trevon's age with eleven years on me. I followed his record religiously once I first saw him play. Elijah's going to be so jealous I met him before he did.

I vaguely recognize the other two people in the room, too. Sonia Holloway commands a powerful presence in her sharp tweed business suit. She's organized a few of the league's charity events I've attended. The other man is her brother, Reid. He entered the NHL at eighteen, but an injury forced him to retire early in his third season.

"Look at his face." Trevon chuckles, slapping me on the back. "Caleb, I'm sure I don't have to introduce Micah to you. Jonesy, this is Caleb Adler."

"It's an honor, sir." I shake his hand, trying—and failing—not to let my inner fanboy out.

Micah chuckles, elbowing Trevon. "Sir. I like this kid already."

"Let's get started, shall we?" Sonia suggests.

"It's good to see you again," I say, taking the seat next to Trevon across from her and her brother. Micah leans against the wall with a cheerful smile.

"First, allow me to reintroduce myself." Sonia holds out a hand to shake. "I'm Sonia Holloway, and this is my brother Reid. We're launching a hockey team based in Mayfield, Massachusetts. You've met our head coach, Micah."

My brows shoot up. Trevon has no idea the gift he's given me.

"Mayfield," I repeat.

She nods. "The Mayfield Mavericks will enter the league next season. When we saw you were available, we knew we had to have you for our roster. I've followed you and your brother's records closely."

I glance at Trevon. He senses where my head's at after working together for so long and jumps in.

"While the circumstances of Mr. Adler's contract with his previous team ending have been embellished and splashed across media outlets, I want to assure you that it was not a reflection of his conduct, professionally or privately," Trevon says.

His way of wording my dismissal from the team over a

difference in morality for the sake of money certainly sounds nicer than the way I'd put it.

"I knew that right away," Sonia says.

"Really?" I sit up straighter.

She nods. "The last time we met, you were in attendance at the fundraising event I organized supporting a hockey night out with patients from a children's hospital. You met with all the children, making sure none were left out, then stayed after to help the staff clean up. You didn't have to do that."

I shrug. "That's the kind of guy I am."

She gives me a sharp, satisfied smirk. "I know. Which is why I haven't believed a word of those articles online. For the record, our PR team tells me fan sentiment is on your side and calling for your teammate to be suspended in light of the eyewitness accounts shared from that night."

Chet would deserve it. I push him from my mind.

Compared to the two previous teams I've been with, I like the energy the three of them bring to the table. It's professional, yet there's an underlying air that's down to earth. It sets me at ease, believing I'm not dealing with people who are only thinking about money.

"This is the offer we've prepared for you." Reid slides a tablet across the table to Trevon.

He puts on a pair of reading glasses and holds it so we both can see. It takes all of my composure to keep my face blank reading the eight figure number. It's triple what I was worth as a player when Seattle signed me.

I was already in, no matter how this meeting went down. It's a hell of a bonus to see a number like that offered for me. I'm ready to ink this deal now, but I wait for my agent to do his thing.

"We believe strongly in the roster we're building and want to make competitive moves to ensure our players feel our sincerity when we say we want to take care of them," Sonia says.

Trevon nods slowly, tapping the four year term length. "Give us five years with a renewal clause for an extension. And add in a no-trade clause."

Reid whispers with Sonia, then nods. "Done."

Trevon looks at me, catching the eager look I'm failing to hold back. He smirks and hands the tablet back.

"I think we're good to go. Send the contract to my office for a full review."

I shake hands with my future team owners and coach. "Thank you."

"Welcome to the Mavs," Micah says.

"Who else is on the roster so far?" I ask.

"We have one other player officially signed," Reid explains. "He's stopping in shortly to finalize everything."

Shortly turns out to be two minutes later. Trevon gets a text and ducks out of the room. He comes back with a familiar face I wasn't expecting to see.

"Is that you, Bouch?" I rise to my feet with a hearty chuckle. "It's been a minute."

Theo Boucher bumps his fist with mine, brown eyes widening in amused delight. He ruffles his hair, the dark blond thicker on top and faded on the sides.

We've known each other since we played on the same team in college. Me and our other teammate, Alex, were both drafted before we finished out our time in the NCAA. Once Theo graduated, he became a free agent and met Trevon through me. We've shared him as an agent ever since and have kept in touch.

"What's up, bro?"

"Is this team a Heston U reunion tour?" I joke.

"They started with the best, obviously," Theo replies.

I snort. "You and Keller were sick wingers. Our line felt unstoppable. I thought you still had a year left in Colorado?"

He shakes his head. "My contract was up for renegotiation, but I was looking for a move to bring me closer to my dad."

I nod in understanding. It becomes crystal clear that my decision to sign with the Mayfield Mavericks is the right one. It keeps me where I want to be with Holly, I respect the ownership, and I'll get to play with an old friend as my teammate once again.

This new team is my opportunity to turn what happened in Seattle with Chet into an inconsequential blip on my player record because I'm far from done with hockey.

"Welcome to the Mavs family," Micah crows. "We're gonna hit it hard next season and build something together."

"Glad to be a part of it," I say.

"Want to grab lunch after this and catch up?" Theo asks.

I grin. "Can't. I've got plans tonight. I'm heading out of the city as soon as I leave here."

"Plans?" He lifts a brow.

"Taking my girlfriend out to dinner to celebrate." It feels damn good to say it.

"Hang on, what girlfriend? You? Since when?" Theo follows me out of the conference room.

My chuckle echoes down the hall. "You'll meet her soon. I'll see you at practice, Bouch."

He claps me on the shoulder. "It's gonna be good to skate with you again."

"Hell yeah."

Two weeks ago, I thought my career was toast. So much has changed for me in that time that I feel like a new man leaving the building. I ride my good mood all the way back to my hotel and hop right in my rental car to hit the road.

CHAPTER 19
CALEB

I DRIVE STRAIGHT to Mayfield from the city, heading for Blissful Bites Bakery to take my girl out. The shop is exactly what I'd picture for Holly's business, the pink cottage exuding her signature charm and style.

"Sorry, man. We're about to clo—Oh. Hey, Caleb." Leo relaxes behind the counter when I enter. "What's up? What are you doing in Mayfield?"

"I'm here to see Holly," I say.

"She's in the back," Leo says. "Through that door."

I nod gratefully when he lets me head for the kitchen. Pausing on the threshold, a soft smile tugs at my lips at the sight of her.

She's laser focused on her work. Her pink hair is swept up in two buns wrapped with thin red bows, and she has another one of her brightly festive aprons on, this one covered in a gingerbread men pattern. Her lip is caught between her teeth as she decorates a set of champagne bottle cookies.

We've only been apart for a little over a day, yet my heart thuds as if it was far longer. I rub my chest and exhale in contentment.

"Hi," I murmur.

Holly freezes. Her gaze rakes over me, lips parting.

I grin, smoothing a hand down my dress shirt. "Do you like the suit?"

She nods, dazed. "Um, yes. Like, a lot." She licks her lips, hastily setting her piping bag aside and dusting flour from her apron. "You look... *Wow*."

"Wow, huh." I can't wipe the broad smile off my face at seeing her so speechless. "Noted."

"Did you come right here from the city?" she asks.

"You bet. I didn't want to be late to pick you up for our date."

I saunter to her, lacing my fingers behind her back and giving her a kiss. She sways into me, then breaks away.

"Wait, I don't want to get your nice suit all dirty. I'm a mess." She checks the time. "The bakery should be closing up. I got wrapped up in working on these because they're being picked up next week. Can you give me a little bit to get ready?"

"You're not a mess. Take all the time you need."

She ducks through the door to talk to her brother, then

blurs past me on her way out the back door. An invisible tether permanently looped around my heart tugs with the desire to follow her.

Instead, I hang in the kitchen and take care of the stuff waiting to be washed in the sink. Folding my suit jacket over a stool, I roll my sleeves up and borrow one of her aprons.

Leo's steps falter behind me when he finds me scrubbing mixing bowls clean. "I was supposed to do that."

I shrug. "I'm waiting for your sister anyway. I've got it."

"Okay. Thanks." He busies himself with storing the cookies Holly was working on.

We work as a team, prepping the bakery for a new day tomorrow. By the time Holly comes back, we've finished. I've got her brother cracking up over a story of how I ended up getting talked into a beer league game for an old teammate's charity event, but got thrown out of the game for tussling with the mascot when he mistook me for his rival from college.

She pauses in the door, surveying the clean kitchen and row of packaged cookies in a basket labeled with the customer's order sheet.

My story cuts off mid-sentence. I'm awestruck by her.

The velvet red dress fits to her curves, flaring out from her waist and falling to her knees. The neckline dips into a point, giving me a tantalizing peek of her cleavage. Her pink hair falls in loose curls, partially pulled back by a sage green bow.

"Wow," I rasp.

She blushes, tucking a curled lock of hair behind her ear. Leo looks between us, popping off the stool.

He fist bumps his sister. "Later."

She admires my forearms. "It looks great in here. Did you help Leo clean up?"

"Yes. You're the one that looks great." I catch her by the waist, thumbs caressing the soft material of her dress. "Ready to go? I made a reservation."

"You did?" She gives me a pleased smile. "Where?"

"There's an inn that had a special winter three-course dinner. I thought you might like it."

Her eyes widen in delight. "The Silver Bell Inn? It's so hard to get a table for their holiday dinners! I've been trying for months because their desserts are to die for."

It was hard to get the reservation. I convinced the concierge to contact the other couple who reserved the table to let them know I wanted to buy them dinner at the most expensive steakhouse in Mayfield. To my relief, they accepted and relinquished their reservation slot to me.

The corner of my mouth lifts. "So I did good, then?"

She smooths her palms up my chest and grabs my shirt collar to pull me down to her level. "You did excellent."

Pressing on tiptoe, she kisses me. My embrace tightens.

When we part, I get my suit jacket and rest my hand on the small of her back on our way out. Everything I want to say to her is ready to spill out of me.

The picturesque inn is decorated like a postcard for the holidays with garlands of pine on the grand porch railings and twinkling lights. Holly releases a tiny excited squeal as I escort her up the steps.

"Look at that." She points above us. "We're under the mistletoe."

I don't need the excuse of mistletoe to kiss her, but I take it anyway because of the way she's smiling up at the decorative floral bundle hanging above us. Time stops existing as we kiss, slowly and full of burning passion.

She keeps her eyes closed, smiling when I pull back. "You know, I don't think I've ever been kissed under the mistletoe before."

"Are you a whole new woman?"

"I might be. How's my hair look?" She poses.

"You're beautiful," I murmur.

Her gaze softens. I treasure her reaction, wanting to make her happy like this all the time.

Inside, we're promptly guided through the intimate rooms set up for diners to our table in a glass conservatory with only two other couples seated.

Holly gasps in amazement. "This is gorgeous!"

I pull her chair out for her, kissing the top of her head once she's scooted in. "Are you warm enough?"

She nods, reading over the menu. "Oh my god, this all sounds delicious. What entree do you think you want out of the three choices we get?"

"Whichever one you want to try. I'll get anything that sounds good to you so you can taste as much as you'd like."

She bites her lip around a pleased smile. "Picking your meal just so I can taste it? You're a real romantic, you know that?"

"Anything for you," I remind her softly.

She makes our wine selection based on the dishes she wants to try. While she's using the restroom, I hand our waiter my credit card and let him know we'd like everything on the menu and cost doesn't matter.

Holly has no idea until all of the options are brought to us. "We didn't order yet."

"I ordered one of everything so we don't have to pick," I explain once the waiter leaves.

Her mouth pops open, then she ducks with a glowing smile. "A girl could get used to this princess treatment."

"Good. You should, because you deserve to be cherished." I pick a plate of seared scallops and offer her a bite first.

Her sparkling eyes lock with mine as her lips wrap around my fork. The corners of her eyes crinkle and she hums with a happy little dance that sends a rush of tenderness through me.

"Good?"

"Yes. Here, you have to try it," she gushes, feeding me a taste.

I hold her eager gaze and accept it. The scallop melts on my tongue.

"Damn, that is nice."

We sample everything, going back for seconds of our favorites. I thoroughly enjoy seeing her having a good time indulging in the decadent flavors of our meal. As we eat, I tell her about my meeting with the Mavericks.

"Wait, the team will be based in Mayfield?" She gapes at me.

"They didn't tell me until today."

"So you'll be here," she says in wonder.

"Right where I want to be—with you."

Her eyes shine. I'm lost in the brilliance of them.

By the time we're done with the main course, she sits back and pats her stomach. We have the conservatory to ourselves after the other two couples finished their meals.

"I'm most excited for the dessert, but I need a breather."

I chuckle, refilling her wine glass first, then mine. "Is she admitting defeat?"

Her lips twitch. "Never. There's always room for dessert."

The lull is the opening I've been waiting all night for. She asked me at the cabin if she could read the note on my phone with the messages I've saved but never sent her. I slide my phone across the table with it open so she can read every word.

"What's this?" She leans forward, eyes flitting across my screen with recognition. "Oh."

"You wanted to know what I wrote to you about." I reach for her hand, covering it with mine as she reads.

A shaky breath tinged with emotion escapes her. She presses her fingers to her lips, her eyes growing misty with unshed tears.

"Caleb." Her whisper encompasses so much—her sentimental reaction, her surprise, her affection for me.

The contents are permanently etched in my mind from my loneliest nights to drunken confessions.

Where are you right now? I'm in Boston. Thinking about driving to you after my game ends. Do you ever think of me? You're on my mind constantly.

A few of my teammates are partying next door with the women they picked up at the bar but I'm in my room alone. I just want to be holding you. I don't want anyone else.

I miss you so fucking much some days I think it's going to eat me alive.

Line after countless line: *I miss you.*

My thumb strokes her hand, swallowing thickly. "I should've had the courage to continue chasing you. Should've sent you these messages and fought for you the way I wanted to. Maybe then we could've been here sooner."

The gruff admission causes a tear to drop down her cheek. I swipe it away and she leans into my palm.

"I'm not making that mistake now. I'll chase you with everything I have, because I don't want to let you go again. You're it for me. Always have been." I gaze into her beautiful eyes and pour my heart out for her. "I love you, Holly. If you're not there yet, that's fine by me. I'll wai—"

"I love you, too," she interrupts in a rush with a wet laugh. "I'm hopelessly gone for you."

My chest swells, the force of it almost knocking me out of my chair. She's made me the happiest damn man in the world.

Astounded by the woman I want to be my wife, I tell her, "I only want a future that has you in it."

Sniffling, she murmurs, "I want that, too. Even if it feels fast, I can't imagine not being with you."

I keep it to myself for the time being that I'm ready to

marry her on the spot if anyone in the restaurant is registered as an officiant.

Lifting her hand to brush with my lips, I wink. "We're not moving fast, sugar. We're catching up."

Holly's no longer the one who got away. She's mine again at last. The cabin was our do over. We've earned our second chance.

CHAPTER 20
HOLLY

AFTER DINNER with my family in Candlewood on Christmas, I stop by the Adler's home for a visit with a treat in hand.

Despite growing up regularly hanging out between my house or Layla's, a bundle of nerves dances in my stomach when I knock on the door. I'm familiar enough to walk in, yet I linger on the doorstep debating how to act when I see Caleb after our date.

My heart swells at the perfect memory. Thinking of those messages he saved makes me misty-eyed again. I copied them to my phone and read some of them again before I got out of my car.

He's made me so happy.

Although he's moving to Mayfield and staying in New England, he's still a professional hockey player. Once the season starts, I can't help wondering if things will be the same as they are now.

I shake my head to dispel the doubt creeping in from the back of my mind.

The door opens, interrupting my thoughts. My heart flutters at the affectionate expression on Caleb's face.

"You came," he says in a mix of surprise, relief, and pleasure.

"I stop by for dessert every year," I answer with a blush, not bringing up how it was only when I knew he wasn't home for the holidays in recent years. "I brought this."

I hold up the extra pecan butter tarts I baked for his family. Thankfully by bribing Leo and Hazel to give me a hand, we were able to make enough of my annual specialty to share with everyone before we closed up the bakery for the holiday and returned to our hometown in Vermont.

The corners of his eyes crinkle. Glancing over his shoulder, he sneaks a hug and a quick kiss before taking my hand to lead me inside. I lick my lips, wishing we could linger in the entryway, just the two of us like our snow globe bubble in the mountains.

He carries the tray for me. It inspires a picture of what our future might look like in another seven years as a couple arriving together to visit family. I bite my lip as butterflies swirl through me.

"You just missed Elijah's call. He's in Toronto since his team's scheduled to play an away series right after the Christmas break," he says.

I slip my hand free from his before we reach the living room where everyone else is. Layla has a crown made of wrapping paper and gift bows. Mr. Adler's cheeks are rosy from drinking and laughing with her. Mrs. Adler bobs her head to the holiday music, waving at me cheerfully.

Layla pops to her feet with a cheer as she runs across the room in a blur of her vivid red hair to hug me. "Holly's here!"

"Merry Christmas." I squeeze her.

Caleb lifts my baked goods out of reach. "I've got dibs. Anyone else want some?"

"Don't you need to get back to the gym to maintain your professional athlete body." She taps him in the stomach with the back of her hand.

He grunts with a smirk, two bites deep. "Can't stop me. Not when it comes to Holly's baking. Shit, these are good. I could eat the entire tray."

A stifled groan of appreciation escapes him. My cheeks heat. I'm unable to control my face, feeling like it's written all over it that I'm in love with him. With effort, I attempt a normal smile.

"They taste different than the last time I had them," he muses curiously.

"I'm glad you like them. Half are the traditional recipe

with brown sugar. Half are maple. I was testing out a twist on the classic to see if I wanted to add them to my bakery's seasonal menu," I say.

Layla finally manages to snag one from Caleb's keep away game, melting as she tastes the pastry. "Oh my god. Mom, Holly made your favorites. They're better than ever."

"Thank you, Holly," Mrs. Adler says.

I smile. "Of course."

I spend time with everyone to hear about their Christmas, finding excuses to be near Caleb. My hand brushes his and we keep sneaking glances.

Afterwards, Layla tugs me away. "Come upstairs. I want to show you my options for New Year's Eve outfits for Girls' Trip: Take Two."

Her bedroom is full of nostalgic memories. K-Pop posters are still plastered on the walls of the groups our friend, Hana, introduced us to in high school. Her massive book collection I still borrow from as a curated taste library. The cozy blanket fort in the corner where we spent most of our sleepovers beneath fairy lights exchanging secrets.

I sit on her bed as she models each option for me. We decide on matching sparkly silver and gold rompers, then plan out a dance playlist to take us to midnight at our private party for two.

I have no doubt Caleb would love to peel the sexy

little number off me at the end of the night. My lips purse to the side. Layla hasn't invited him to come with us. He might be busy with training once he's signed with his new hockey team, anyway.

Maybe next year we'll get to spend New Year's Eve together and I'll get to kiss my boyfriend when the clock strikes twelve. At the very least, I'll call him to hear his voice while I'm at the cabin.

After our time there, the thought of going back without him strikes a sharp chord in me.

The cabin might be his family's, but in my heart it will forever be branded as our space from now on.

By the time we return downstairs, I'm bursting with the need to tell my best friend about falling for her brother.

Except I don't have to worry about finding the right words to tell her. Instead, Caleb waits for us at the foot of the staircase.

The story Layla's telling trails off as he catches me by the waist and pulls me in for a kiss when I reach the last step, easy as that.

Wide-eyed and flushed, I press my fingers to my lips. I can't believe he did that. My attention flies to his smiling sister behind me. She nudges me to get me moving again.

"You don't seem surprised about your brother randomly coming up and kissing me," I say.

Layla gestures between us with her brow quirked.

"Well, yeah. There's been an obvious vibe going on between you two since you got here. I can see how he's looking at you, and the glances you've been sneaking at him. You both have no idea what subtlety is."

"Oh. I didn't mean to hide it from you, but I wasn't sure when to tell you about us," I say.

"I'm happy you two finally got your heads out of your asses," she replies with a laugh. "Seriously, me and Eli had bets going for years on who would crack first."

Caleb snorts and hugs me against his side, right where I belong. We fit perfectly together. I lean my head on his shoulder, not fighting the soft smile that breaks free.

"Who had money on seven years ago?" he asks.

Layla gasps, pointing at us. "I knew it! For the record, you two suck at sneaking around."

My mouth pops open. "There's no way you suspected us. We were careful."

She shakes her head. "Yeah, sweetie, no. You weren't as discreet as you thought." She tallies on her fingers. "June, his car smelled like your perfume. My family's July 4th barbecue, you both disappeared around the same time and I found one of your bows from your braids that day in a bush. Two weeks after that, I heard you laughing in his room—I've known you since we were kids, so, duh, I'd recognize it. Should I keep going?"

"Oh my god. You have more?" I turn my mortified face into Caleb's chest.

"Your brain is something to be feared if you're pissed off," he says to his sister. "How do you remember shit like that?"

Layla taps her temple. "I am an iron vault. I see all. I archive all. This is why you and Eli could never beat me at games like hide and seek, because I memorized all your best spots."

He chuckles wryly. "This is why you never mess with the middle child."

"Damn right," Layla crows.

"You never said anything. I'm sorry for keeping it from you back then." I pull away from Caleb to hug my best friend.

She squeezes me back fiercely. "Don't sweat it, girl. I wasn't mad at all. I was hyped, because our childhood bestie dream of becoming sisters might come true. Then I was pissed at him for whatever he did to make you so sad at the end of the summer."

"Oh, is that why you were suddenly giving me so much attitude and ignored me when I was home on break from school?" Caleb scoffs.

Layla flips him off. "Oh, you hush."

"Give me my girlfriend back." His hands snake around my waist and tug me into his chest.

Layla holds on. "She was my friend first."

"Play nice, children. Hey—wait, don't tickle me!" I yelp.

The three of us wrestle, stifling uncontrollable laughter. Layla plays dirty jabbing her brother in the side, but he wins out in the end by scooping me into his arms. I cling to him and throw my head back with joyful amusement.

If this is my future, I look forward to every minute of it.

CHAPTER 21
HOLLY

THE LAST OF the holiday rush between Christmas and New Year's has me a bit on edge. Blissful Bites is behind on orders and there are fires to put out from when I was gone. The first day back after I drop Leo off at his college campus, I don't stop moving longer than thirty seconds all day.

I'm truly grateful for Leta and my siblings' extra help covering the bakery on short notice while I was snowed in, and to thank them I paid them all bonuses on top of their paychecks.

As I get back into my routine, I'm finding things taking me longer than usual when supplies are out of place, ingredients haven't been replenished, and the shop is slammed with customers out enjoying the holidays in Mayfield's historic shopping district.

The goal is to reorganize the bakery, catch up on the orders waiting in the queue, and have my shop running in smooth order once again by the end of the day.

Oh, and remember to feed myself somewhere in the spare moments between.

Leo's off for the rest of the week, enjoying what's left of his winter break from college, and Hazel's home in Candlewood. Leta's on vacation with her family, so I'm the only one here.

The challenge doesn't intimidate me. I'll just have to work harder.

I'm accustomed to handling most things on my own. I used to believe it was faster if I shouldered everything myself. I'd always think, if I could figure out how to multiply myself, I'd be set for life.

At some point, it grew more challenging to count on others, instilling a strong sense that I'm being a burden to people if I can't do something on my own without them.

I don't want to delegate and explain every little thing I need done. But...it would be nice if I could.

According to Leo, the standards I set for myself are considered high and unrealistic whenever I remind him how I like things to be packaged.

And maybe that's my problem with knowing when I can't do it all by myself. I put these rigid expectations on myself and fear what happens when I don't achieve them.

I can't go on like this forever, or I'll skate too close to running myself into the ground.

The tight way I grip the reins of control now that I'm in my usual routine makes me starkly aware of how much better things were for me tucked away at the cabin when I had Caleb to rely on.

With him, I never feel like I'd be troubling him if I reached out. It's the complete opposite.

It was so nice to have someone who sensed whatever I might want before I voiced it. He took care of me in a way I've never been looked after before.

He's the one I need to remind me he's there to catch me when my independent nature finally exhausts me.

Unfortunately, I can't expect to have him here all the time. But thanks to him, I'm starting to see I should learn to be better about realizing I sometimes require support from others without my irrational worry of pushing my problems onto them.

These old habits of mine are tough to break.

Once I'm immersed in work, I take on more and more until I overload myself, determined to handle it all.

I hope I don't come off a little unhinged in front of my customers. Between putting batches of treats in the oven, setting timers, and working the counter with a dazzling smile—all while whispering to myself to keep track of my to-do list so I don't forget a thing—I'm a human whirlwind decked out in pink.

It's worth every second of madness when I see people enjoying my baked goods and hanging out in my homey, comforting space. Watching their expressions light up at the treats I've lovingly baked is everything to me.

It never gets old and never fails to brighten my spirits. From the time I taught myself to bake and first saw my younger siblings enjoying what I made to now running my shop, it warms my heart. I love what I do.

By the end of the day, I've made a good dent in what I have left for the New Year's Eve party cookie order, rearranged my restocked ingredient shelf so my most-used things are back in place, and I sold out of everything I made for the day. I still have to catch up on other orders that have piled up, but I extinguished the most pressing fires.

I'm about to fall asleep on my aching feet, but I did it. A tired, successful smile tugs at my lips.

Once I lock up the front of the shop, I trudge to the back with a yawn, gathering my things to head home for the night.

A steaming mug of hot chocolate, a holiday movie marathon, and a kiss from the most handsome hockey player I know would fix me. I just know it would.

At least the first two are in my immediate future as soon as I go up to my apartment above the shop and take the hottest, most luxurious shower of my life to wash away my stress. I text Caleb before I leave the bakery.

. . .

HOLLY

Longest day ever is over. I got so much
done! Time for fuzzy slippers.

CALEB

I'm proud of you, sugar. Sounds like
you've earned a massage.

HOLLY

Oh my god, that sounds so nice. A
massage might bring me back to life
right now.

CALEB

You don't have to ask. My hands are all
yours.

HOLLY

I'm going up to my apartment to take a
shower, but I'll call you after if you're not
asleep yet.

When I exit into the alley behind the block of shops, I halt
in my tracks.

Caleb's crouched to pet one of the cats Marjorie, the
bookstore owner, feeds. He tilts his head and gives me a
charming dimpled smile.

"Hi beautiful," he murmurs.

"Wait—I thought you went back to your hotel after

touring the practice rink for the Mavs." I glance from my phone to him. "What are you doing here?"

"Waiting for you. I came to make sure you get home safe."

A warm glow fills me from within at his heartfelt tone and expression.

"I don't have far to go. You want to walk me upstairs?" I tease.

"I want you," he replies.

I can't help the grin that breaks free when he gathers me in his strong arms and presses me against the building for a sweeping kiss.

All my stress melts away once I'm in his embrace. I worry too much when I'm left to my own thoughts, but when he holds me I no longer feel the weight of everything I carry.

I sigh, grazing my nose against his. "I don't do well with surprises from others. But from my boyfriend? I understand the appeal."

"Call me your boyfriend again. I like the sound of it," he rasps.

I suppress a shiver. "I think I like having you waiting for me after work."

"Yeah? That's good. You should get used to it." His lips brush mine again.

"Ah, but if I do, how will I survive without it when you're on the road for away games?" I wrap my arms around his shoulders. "Cake. Cake makes everything better. And I suppose I have my vibrator to keep me company whenever you're gone."

He buries his face in my neck with a smoky rumble. "I'm going to buy you one of those ones for couples to use over long distances. It doesn't matter where I am, I'll always make you come."

I bite my lip, tipping my head back to give him better access. My breath hitches as his hands wander beneath my sweater. Since I live above the shop, I don't bother with a coat.

"If you don't take me home, we're going to scandalize the other shopkeepers and Marjorie's cat army," I warn.

"You're too hard to resist," he protests against my skin.

I giggle, pushing against his chest. He straightens, cupping my cheek and flashing me a wry tilt of his mouth.

"Can I walk you home?" he offers.

"Please. Will you stay the night?"

"I was hoping you'd ask."

His hand rests on my lower back and he takes my over-stuffed tote bag from me, eyeing the keychain clipped to the handle with my bakery keys, apartment key, and an assortment of plushie charms with a twitch of his lips.

Upstairs in my apartment, he tugs me down next to him on the couch. I curl against his side, humming with gratitude as he pulls my feet in his lap and makes good on his massage offer.

"This beats the hotel room any day," he says.

"Did you find any nice places when you drove around this morning?" I ask.

"I did. It's near here. Nice neighborhood." He winks.

"Oh, I think I'm getting a new neighbor. Marjorie came by for her afternoon treat and said someone wanted to lease the empty place above her bookstore. They move in this weekend, apparently."

His mouth spreads into a grin. I incline my head, squinting as he grows more amused and proud of himself. There's no way he means he's the one who—?

Chuckling, he kisses the top of my head. "Meet your new neighbor, sugar cookie. I wanted to be as close to you as possible. Just my luck the place next door was available, right?"

"You're ridiculous." I shake my head, cheeks aching with the strength of my smile.

"Yeah, but you like it," he reminds me.

"I do, don't I?" I snuggle against him.

"That's right, baby."

As we spend the night laughing and cuddling on the couch, I've found my new perfect snow globe for the two of us to exist in.

CHAPTER 22
CALEB

Training won't begin until the team roster for the Mavericks is filled. It doesn't mean I can't keep my conditioning up. I meet up with Theo in the morning to hit the gym, then we go for an afternoon skate at our new practice rink.

"Three weeks off from the ice and you're going soft on me," Theo jokes when he finishes a skating drill before me.

I grab my water bottle off the boards and squirt it into my mouth, huffing. "Okay, maybe I went a little hard on the baked goods during my time keeping my head down from the shitty PR storm."

"That's on you for dating a bakery owner."

"And I wouldn't change a damn thing about it," I shoot back with a grin. "Except the dating part. That's my future wife you're talking about."

It feels fucking good to say it. *My wife.* I can't wait to call Holly that.

The minute I think she's ready, I'm putting my ring on her finger. I already started shopping around for the perfect one worthy of my sparkling girl.

Theo smirks, shaking his head. "You and Alex are the same. All obsessed and shit. That's not my style. I'll stick to hook ups only."

I match his expression. "You say that now. Then the right one comes along and boom—" I thump the front of his jersey with my fist over his heart. "—you're a goner."

"Nah. Not for me."

"I look forward to the day you meet someone who makes you eat those words," I taunt with a chuckle.

We move away from the boards. Theo collects a puck with his stick from the pile we dumped by the net and starts a one on one scrimmage against me.

The last time we faced off with each other was years ago during a showcase game. Most of the times our old teams played each other during the regular season, we were on different lines and never saw time on the ice as opponents in an official game.

He skates in circles around me with clean edge work that stokes a competitive fire in my chest. The drive that made me strive for this career with everything I had to give reawakens.

I get serious and push myself, stealing the puck and flying down the ice. Theo whoops and hauls ass after me.

With him breathing down my neck, I take the shot on the net, crowing with my fist in the air when it sails into the crease.

I feel fucking alive again. Exhilaration and determination pump through my veins. My love for the game is unshakable.

Sitting out of the rest of this season will be worth it when opening night rolls around in October.

We go a few more rounds, each of us bagging a win. I haven't had this much fun in ages. Probably as far back as my college days.

I'm drenched in sweat by the time we finish. My damp hair curls against my forehead. I shake it out and slick it back as we skate to the boards.

Theo downs half his water bottle and nudges my phone. "Your brother texted. How is he? I miss that kid."

"He's good. Did you see his game last night?"

"Hell yeah. I taught him how to make that beauty of a shot when he was a rookie," he boasts.

"No, I taught him how when he was learning how to skate on my grandparents' pond." My brows jump up as I grab my phone and read Elijah's message and a shocked scoff escapes me. "Oh shit."

"What is it?"

"You know how Sonia set me up with a meeting to talk

to the team's PR manager? I got the go ahead to make a statement on what happened with Chet at that bar."

It felt good to speak out about Chet's character and my belief that he—and anyone like him who disregards a woman's consent or is a danger to women in any way—has no place in hockey or any other sport. Organizations shouldn't be protecting or making any kind of concessions for them, either.

The post I made yesterday has thousands of likes and too many comments agreeing with me to keep up with.

"This article Elijah sent me says he's being put on the inactive list pending investigation by the league after charges were brought against him from another incident he was involved in last year."

Theo gives a low whistle. "I hope he's kicked out of the league."

"It's what he deserves. Guys like him don't belong in hockey."

"Damn right. Ready to call it and hit the showers?"

"Sounds good."

He smirks, skating backwards towards the exit to the locker room once we've cleaned up the equipment. "Are we getting a bite to eat after this?"

I chuckle, jostling him when I skate by. "I'm going home to my girl."

"No teammate bonding? No love for your buddy?" He

messes around with me by gripping my jersey and making me tow him.

"Not as much as I love her."

I stroll through the crowd of post-holiday shoppers, eager to get home to Holly at the bakery. As I sidestep to move out of the way for an elderly couple, something in the antique store's display window catches my eye.

A snow globe. The base has ceramic pink bows circling it and if I'm not mistaken, there's a cabin scene inside. Immediately, I think of Holly.

The bell rings when I enter the store to buy it for her. My nose tickles with the urge to sneeze at the aged scent clinging to the air.

I find the snow globe, pleased to find it is a cabin along with a small figurine of a couple waving in front of it. With a shake, white flurries swirl inside along with flakes of pink and gold glitter. It's perfect.

"Do you know any recommendations where I can get this engraved?" I ask while purchasing it.

"The jewelry store two doors down offers a personalization service," the clerk answers.

"Thank you."

Gift in hand, I find the jewelry store and drop it off for engraving before I head to the bakery.

It's as packed as the busy sidewalk outside. There's a line at the counter six people deep and a few tables have empty plates.

I collect them and wipe the tables down, helping a mother slide two of the tables together for her children to eat at.

Holly doesn't spot me right away, too occupied taking care of her customers. When she does, she spares me a quick smile and a wave before getting back to it.

"Are you out of these maple cookies?" The man placing his order taps the empty spot in the display case.

Holly presses on her tiptoes to see. "It looks like I am. Sorry about that, I didn't realize the last one sold. If you'll wait just a moment, I've got a fresh batch about to come out of the oven. How many would you like?"

"Three," he decides.

She plasters on a smile and rings him up. "I'll be back in a sec."

It's not her real, effortless smile. I rub at the hot sensation irritating my chest.

It drives a wedge through me seeing her pushing herself to the brink like this. Tired. Overwhelmed. Fighting on her own to keep it all in check.

She's not alone. She has me at her side.

I'm filled with the need to take the weight she carries from her before she needs to ask. I want to do this for her every day for the rest of our lives.

I'll become the support she can trust will always be there for her to lean on from here on out.

Without a word, I step behind the counter as she ducks into the back and sanitize my hands at the sink. I greet the next customer in line with a friendly smile.

"How's it going today? What can I get started for you?"

"Two chocolate muffins," the woman replies.

"Coming right up." I grab the tongs in the case and bag the muffins before ringing up the total with the touch-screen display.

Holly falters in the doorway when she returns, giving me a glassy-eyed look that makes me want to wrap her in my arms and protect her from the entire world.

We work in tandem through the rest of the line. Once it's calmed down, I sweep the shop again to bus the tables and take the dirty dishes to the kitchen to wash. Before starting them, I message Layla.

CALEB

You don't start your new job until after New Year's once you're at your new place in Mayfield, right?

LAYLA

Yup. Mom's made an excuse to go shopping every day. She's sad I'm leaving her. It's not like I'm going far [laughing emoji]

CALEB

Then you're free this week?

LAYLA

Why, what's up?

CALEB

We could use a hand at Holly's. She won't admit it yet, but I want to call in reinforcements for her.

LAYLA

Done!!! My girl needs me? I'm there.

CALEB

See if Mom is free too. Do you have her family's numbers?

LAYLA

I'm on it. Leave operation bestie support squad to me.

CALEB

Thank you.

LAYLA

I'm really glad she has you. She needs someone who can love her right.

CALEB

That's all I want to do.

LAYLA

What happened in that cabin?

CALEB

I'm not telling you that.

LAYLA

I'm just curious. You seem serious.

CALEB

I am. She's it for me.

LAYLA

Sooooo... should I expect certain shiny news in the future? [Ring emoji]

CALEB:

[smirk emoji]

LAYLA

Caleb!!!!!!

She sends a short video of herself shrieking and running around in excitement. Tucking my phone away with a satisfied huff of amusement, I roll my sleeves up and wash the dishes.

Not long after, Holly comes in and plops on a stool. "Today was nonstop. But I made it to closing time without a breakdown. Score."

I finish drying the plates with a frown. "As an athlete I understand mental stress, but I don't think that's a win if you're pushing yourself too hard."

She waves me off. "I'm fine. Just being dramatic."

Stacking the dishes, I start wiping down the work tables and listen while she talks.

"This is the bakery's first full year being open through the holidays, so I'm learning a lot. Next year I think I should bring in extra part-timers to manage the front."

"That sounds like a good idea."

She slides off her seat and attempts to help me clean up. I encourage her back to it to relax, but she spins to face me.

"The holiday rush is great for business, but I barely had time to do anything today. The cookie order I started this morning never got decorated. Can you believe I almost burnt my cinnamon rolls twice trying to multitask, and—"

I lock my arms around her mid sentence. She stills, then softens, melding against me.

"Thank you," she murmurs into my chest.

"For what?"

"Helping."

My arms tighten. "You know if you need help, it's okay to ask? You don't have to do it all on your own."

She nods, then wriggles closer. "I want to just stay like this."

My chin rests on her head. "I'm not letting go."

"I still have two more designs to finish for the big party order." She sighs, pulling back. "Maybe I should tell Layla we could have our New Year's here instead."

I catch her hand, bringing it to my lips for a kiss. "Planning to work all night?"

Her expression is caught out. "Um..."

"It's time for a break."

She appears like she's going to fight me. Is that how it is? I can deal with this.

The corner of my mouth lifts and I throw her over my shoulder. She clings to the back of my shirt, laughing. The lighthearted sound eases my concern for her.

"Caleb!"

"No arguing, sugar. You're done with work for the day."

Holly gives in, instructing me how to close the bakery for the night when I refuse to let her down because I know she'll find something to do.

After locking up, I carry her upstairs to her apartment and spend the rest of the night pampering the shit out of my future wife. First, by making her dinner and washing her hair when we shower, then by worshipping her with my tongue until she's thoroughly ravished.

CHAPTER 23
HOLLY

I FINALLY ASSURE myself it's okay to ask for help. Because after working my ass off yesterday at the bakery, I need it or I'm going to burn out. This detrimental habit of mine is born from a combination of independence and an unfortunate inability to receive assistance without feeling like I owe someone twofold for lending a hand.

Honestly, I'm struggling. It's still difficult for me to acknowledge it, even to myself.

I get so wrapped up in my work that I don't notice I'm drowning in it until the water's high above my head and I'm too exhausted to keep swimming.

Sometimes it's not feasible to stubbornly do everything alone.

And that's okay. I'm coming to terms with the realization and set a goal for myself to work on it.

Caleb's the one who helped me accept that I'm not inconveniencing others by needing their help.

I don't have to rely on myself alone. I have people in my life who are there for me as much as I am for them.

I'm proud of what I've accomplished by opening Blissful Bites Bakery. It's my baby I've built with all of my passion poured into it from the start. I want to see it continue to grow.

However, something I've learned in the last few weeks is that it's different running the shop compared to the made-to-order online business I started in college. I only had to worry about what I was making for the orders I took, not a whole menu on top of them and serving customers.

It all runs through my head during the night while I'm snuggled in Caleb's arms. I slept for a short while, utterly shattered by his devoted attention after he took me home. Once I was awake, my brain wouldn't stop turning over everything on my to-do list.

He gives a protesting grumble, holding me tighter when I slip out of bed long before the sun rises. I bend to kiss him and run my fingers through his unruly hair until he falls asleep again, smiling softly at the way he hugs my pillow.

As I spend my favorite time of day on my own with my thoughts, I make up my mind. By the time I've had coffee and go downstairs to the shop, I have a plan to check with my friends and family to see who might be around.

Layla might not be busy and Leo did insist I should let him know if I needed him to come in. My parents haven't been to Mayfield for a visit lately, and Mom did mention wanting to come down for a day trip to grab lunch with me and stroll the shopping district.

Familiar eldest daughter guilt momentarily bubbles up at making plans with any of them because I need their help, but I stop it in its tracks. They're my family and I should be able to count on them the same way they can depend on me.

I make a sign for the front door to change the shop hours to give myself time to manage one task at a time. The order queue takes priority for now.

As I work on the one I started yesterday, Caleb comes down. He hugs me from behind while I'm mixing meringue powder into the royal icing recipe. His big hands slip beneath my apron, splaying on my soft stomach.

"Morning," he says gruffly.

"Morning was two hours ago for me," I tease.

He tucks his face against the crook of my neck with a hum. "Did you eat?"

"I had coffee."

"That's not food."

"It's a necessity," I declare.

His husky laugh tickles my skin. "Where are the eggs? I'll make you something."

Pleasure sweeps through me at the domestic intimacy. Mornings are my peaceful sanctuary, but I like them better when he's part of them. His presence is a reassuring blanket wrapped around me.

"Here. Take a short break to eat your breakfast." He guides me away from the standing mixer to sit and feeds me the first bite of food.

"Thank you." I take the plate.

He presses his lips to the top of my head. "I'm going to pick up coffee while I run an errand. Do you want more?"

"Yes, please."

I tilt my head back for a kiss. He gives it to me, smiling into it.

"I'll be back in a little bit," he says.

After eating, I check my phone. It's reached a decent time of day for the rest of the world who didn't rise before dawn to work in a bakery.

I brush my hands off on my apron and take a breath. I tell my overreacting nerves that I'm reaching out to my friend for help, not running from a predator, so there's no reason whatsoever for my fight-or-flight response to kick up over a phone call.

I push down the jumpy anxiousness that comes with putting myself out there rather than handling things by myself and call Layla. She answers on the first ring.

"Good morning, sunshine," she chirps.

"You're up early. And super chipper. Did you get laid?" I guess.

"God, I wish," she laments.

"New Year's resolution?" I suggest.

"Only if I find someone who's hot, rich, and gives me princess treatment," she fires back with a scoff.

There's a deep murmur from someone nearby. Her voice muffles to shush them. I lift a brow, wondering who she's with.

"Anyway, what's up?" she asks.

I pad into the front of the shop, fluffing the pillows on the window seat and adjusting the decorations.

"Oh, I'm just calling because I was wondering if you might be around. I thought maybe you'd want to come stay with me for a couple of days before we..."

The front door opens, making me trail off. Caleb returns with two filled trays of coffee—and his sister.

"Layla?" I stare from her to my phone, the call still connected. "You didn't tell me you were in town."

"Surprise." She wiggles her fingers with a beaming grin, then hugs me.

Caleb holds the door open and I'm stunned into silence as more people walk in. My brother ambles through the door, absorbed in his phone. He nods to me nonchalantly with his chin. Then my parents and sister, followed by Mrs. Adler.

"Hi, sweetheart." Dad kisses my cheek.

"Hi. You're here," I stammer.

"Of course we are. This'll be fun," Hazel says.

"There's plenty of coffee for everyone," Caleb says.

"Let's get this party started," Layla announces.

Hazel removes the sign I made for the door and goes into the back. Layla hooks her arm with Leo as he heads for the kitchen behind my sister. My parents and Mrs. Adler follow them. I overhear Leo delegating tasks.

"When—how did everyone know I needed—?" I turn to Caleb, knees weak at his handsome features set in a sincere expression.

"I called in reinforcements for you," he murmurs.

"For me?" I reply faintly.

His cheek dimples with the curve of his mouth. He draws me close, cupping my cheek. His warm green gaze bounces between mine, dancing with boundless affection that steals my breath.

"For you, sugar. Because I'll always do anything for you."

He brushes his lips against mine, making my heart flutter from the tender kiss. I sway into him, hugging my arms tightly around his waist. When we part, I blink away the tears watering my eyes.

"Thank you for always knowing what I need. Somehow, you have a super power to do it before I'm even aware of it," I say in awe.

His smile broadens. "Because I pay attention so I can take care of you. I'm here for you, and so is everyone else. Not because that's what the holidays are all about, but any time you need. Whether you reach out or not, I'll catch you."

I bite my lip, chest swelling at his sincerity. He's given me the greatest gift by removing worries from my plate with his thoughtful support.

Bright, twinkling happiness rushes through me, overflowing endlessly.

"I love you, Caleb," I say.

He exhales in contentment, closing his eyes. "Say it again?"

Tugging him down by his collar, I speak against his lips. "I love you." *Kiss.* "I love you." *Kiss.* "I love—"

He cuts me off, sealing his mouth over mine with a playful growl.

"If you two are done making out, we've got a bakery to run," Layla says from the doorway.

Laughing, I rest my forehead against his. He steals one more kiss, ignoring his sister's ribbing.

Revitalized by how cherished Caleb's surprise makes me feel, I can't wait to get to work.

All of us come together, working alongside one another. With Leo, Hazel, and Mrs. Adler's help, I'm able to get ahead on the order queue. While we make hundreds of cookies, Layla and Mom run the front counter and Dad handles the dishes all day.

Caleb fills in wherever an extra hand is needed, and whenever I catch his eye he's watching me, proud and adoring.

Later, after we've all gone out for dinner together, Caleb walks me home hand in hand. The row of shops is lit with twinkling lights. Light snow begins falling.

"Look, it's our good luck charm," he says.

"The snow?" I tease.

He grins. "Sure. It got us our second shot. When you win, you hold on to whatever takes you there."

I fight an enchanted smile. "Is this another hockey player thing?"

His smile widens in response. I shake my head, shoulders shaking.

"You're such a goof."

"And you love it." He tugs me closer, putting an arm around my waist to hug me.

"I do. Can't be helped."

"I got you something," he says.

"You did?"

"That was my errand earlier. I was picking up your belated Christmas present."

I lean into him. "You didn't have to."

"I wanted to," he counters.

"Surprising me with our families today was a gift all on its own."

We reach the bakery and head up to my apartment. I imagine once Caleb moves into the one next door above the book store, we'll be sharing both spaces.

He draws me down to the couch once our coats are discarded, offering the gift bag he returned with after picking up coffee this morning.

"Here. Open it."

I gasp when I pull a snow globe from the cocoon of tissue paper. It's so much like the one I love at his family's cabin, the large glass dome creating a magical bubble around a cozy cabin. The only difference is this one has two tiny figurines waving in front of the cabin.

"It's beautiful," I whisper.

"I'm glad you like it," he rasps.

"I love it."

An inscription on the base between the ceramic pink bows catches my eye.

Always together with you, sugar.

I bite my lip and trace the engraved words with my fingertips. Turning it over, my breath hitches in appreciation at the beautiful snow and glitter swirling inside.

"This made me think of you. It's you and me. Side by

side through any storm and the calm that follows," he says as the decorative flurries settle.

He covers my hands with his, holding the gift between us. I meet his reverent gaze, butterflies filling my stomach.

"I want to be in every snow globe with you, as long as we're together."

I swallow thickly, nodding. Setting the gift aside carefully, I melt against him, winding my arms around his shoulders as we kiss.

His hands run down my spine, pulling me against him. I straddle his lap, tearing my mouth from his only long enough to strip my sweater off.

He trails kisses across the tops of my breasts while deftly unhooking the clasp of my bra. As he peels it off me, he peers up at me as if I'm a goddess to be worshiped.

I slide my fingers over his jaw, mapping the masculine shape and his stubble. He tips his head back for me, never taking his eyes off me. I press my lips to his, gentle and sweet, then harder and more demanding. He makes a gravelly sound that reverberates from his chest, stirring my need for him.

In a smooth display of strength that makes me gasp, he grips my ass and lifts me as though I'm weightless to him when he pushes to his feet. He carries me to the bedroom without breaking the kiss.

Laying me out gently on the bed, he loses his shirt and kneels over me, kissing a line down my stomach. My fingers sink in his hair as he rubs his cheek against my abdomen.

There's no urgency in our movements. We linger in every touch, savoring each other.

He strips us both bare. His skin is warm against mine when he fits himself between my legs. For a while, we kiss without an end goal, our limbs tangled.

We rock our hips together until I can't hold back from how good it feels with his hard length rubbing me with each languid movement.

"I need you," I plead.

"I've got you," he promises, caressing my cheek.

He shifts his weight onto his forearm and lines up where I want him most. Both of us sigh as he sinks inside me inch by inch. He fills me so perfectly, I cry out. Hushing me, he loops my arms around his neck and starts to move.

"I'll never get enough of you," he says against my jaw.

"Me either," I say breathlessly.

"Hold on to me, sugar."

I tighten my arms around his neck, never wanting to let go of him again.

He keeps the same slow pace with harder snaps of his hips that set me ablaze. Hazy gasps of his name slip from me as I lock my legs around him for more. He squeezes the underside of my thigh.

"Come with me," he rasps.

I kiss him. His grip on my trembling leg spasms and his thrusts become sharper, bringing me to the brink.

We fall over the edge together, swept up in one another.

Once we recover, he gives me a charming smile. I touch the dimple in his cheek. He turns his face into my hand, kissing my palm with gentle, affectionate murmurs. The loving swell of my heart is never-ending.

In his arms, I'm finally right where I've always belonged.

EPILOGUE

CALEB

TEN MONTHS LATER

THE NIGHT I've been waiting for all year has finally arrived—opening night for the hockey season. We have our first regular season game on home ice at the arena downtown.

I'm fired up to get out there and play with the teammates who have become like brothers to me over the last several months.

The Mayfield Mavericks team launch made a big splash across sports media outlets. This time, the PR frenzy didn't send me into hiding.

The place is packed when I walk by the tunnel with Theo on our way to the locker room after warming up our muscles. He pauses, tapping my shoulder with his knuckles.

"Damn, sounds like the entirety of Mayfield showed up to watch us play."

"Yeah. We better give them something to cheer about."

He eyes me with a smirk, giving me a light shove. "I know that dopey ass look. You only care about one person yelling your name tonight."

"Tonight and every night."

He snorts. I grin, scanning the limited view of the lower bowl from the tunnel for my girl with the other WAGs.

Holly's my girlfriend now, but there's no doubt in my mind: she's my future wife. Soon enough, I'll finally give her the ring I bought months ago.

He grabs me by the back of my collar and drags me away. "Come on, lover boy. You'll see her soon enough when we hit the ice."

The other guys are going through their own stages of physical and mental preparation prior to a game. I pop a pair of headphones in my ears and sit on the bench at my locker to tape my stick while visualizing my goals.

Before Holly came back into my life, my visualization techniques focused solely on gameplay and running through the skills I worked hard to hone.

Now, I picture everything in my life I want to play for. I'm no longer dedicated to my job by my love of the sport alone, but driven by the good things that make me happier than I've ever been. It's a way to unload anything I should let go of before the puck drops, leaving me focused.

Tonight might be my first game back since my contract was terminated midseason last year, but I'm playing better than ever. My reaction time is flawless and I chase the puck with everything I've got because I'm not holding back in my life anymore.

I've felt it in training this year, but I know it once I step on the ice—I'm unstoppable tonight.

I'm locked in, ready to win against our opponents.

Fans shout my name when I skate around the edge of the rink to get my legs ready. I wave, tossing a few pucks to kids with homemade signs.

At last, I spot my girl standing at the glass to watch warm-ups when I reach the section she's sitting in a few rows up with the other players' partners and Layla. My sister gives me a wave from her seat.

"Watch out. Hot heartbreaker alert," Holly says.

She's filming me on her phone and blows me a kiss. I catch it with my glove and tuck it against my heart, giving her a wink.

Pieces of her hair are pulled up in two spots, tied with blue bows to match the team colors. Best of all, she's wearing my jersey. She sewed on glittery pink beads to add hearts to it.

I'll never tire of seeing her wearing my name and number. She's mine for life.

"You look good." My gaze rakes over her.

She spins, showing off the back of the jersey. "Oh, you like it?"

"You in my jersey? Fuck yes." My voice lowers just enough that she'll still hear it through the glass dividing us. "I'll like it even better when it's the only thing you have left on later."

Her cheeks redden and she plucks the material for emphasis. "I wanted to let everyone here know that's my man scoring out there."

"Yours and only yours. Know that every puck I put in the net is all for you," I promise.

Theo skates by, busting my balls. "Game time, lover boy."

Grinning, I hold up my glove against the glass. Holly puts hers against the other side.

"See you after."

"You've got this!"

Her confidence in me fires me up. I push off the boards and ride the boost all the way to puck drop when the game begins.

I win the first face-off against Pittsburgh.

It feels damn good moving the puck down the ice passing to Theo and Howell as they flank me. Howell's shot on the net gets blocked, but Theo picks up the rebound and out skates Pittsburgh's defense.

His deke to me works in his favor and he sends a wrister across the goal line for our first point.

"Hell yeah!" He pumps his fist in the air, bumping it against mine between plays.

My line completely dominates the game every time our shift is up. I haul myself over the boards and don't stop moving until it's time for the next line to take over. When I'm out, I'm watching gameplay like a hawk.

We're up by one point going into third period and I don't want to give up the lead.

Pittsburgh fights us hard, not ready to call it quits during the last minutes of the game. We're locked in a brutal back and forth that takes us from one end of the rink to the other. Neither team scores.

Howell and one of our D-men get the puck far enough out to give us an advantage.

"Go!" I yell, flying with them.

Howell flicks the puck to me before he's checked. Pittsburgh's center slams into me. I move the puck to Theo and get to the scoring zone.

Theo passes back to me when I'm open with seconds to spare on the clock. Defense is creeping in on my right to close off my options for an easier shot.

I don't back down yet, my muscles burning with

instinctive competitiveness. The goalie thinks I'm going left.

Smirking, I angle to make it look like I am, changing directions at the last second to drive the puck down the center when the goalie slides to the spot he thought I'd shoot from. The puck sails past him into the crease.

The lamp lights up and the crowd goes wild.

Dazed as adrenaline courses through me, I stare at the final score. 3-0. A fucking shutout for our first official game.

Holy shit. I haven't played a shutout in—christ, I can't remember. Not when I was on either of the other NHL teams I played for.

Theo crashes against me, followed by the rest of our teammates piling on us in celebration. I laugh with them, proud to be playing with each of them.

After showering and getting through postgame interviews and a debrief with the coaches, I meet up with Holly and Layla in the suite where family and friends hang out. The team's having a private after party for opening night nearby.

Layla high fives me. "He's back, baby."

"I am." And it feels fucking good.

"That was an incredible game," Holly gushes.

The thrill that fires through me hearing her say that is almost strong enough to knock me down. Taking her hand, I lead the girls to my car to drive us over to the party. Our fingers lace together and they chat animatedly on the way to the parking lot.

My parents text their congratulations in the family group chat. Elijah's team is still playing their game when I check for the final score.

The drive to the party isn't long. A few of the other guys are already there.

"This place is nice," Layla says.

Humming in agreement, my hand rests at Holly's back. "The team's owners take good care of us."

A live band plays before a dance floor and the walls are lined with intimately lit green velvet booths.

We order drinks and my teammates flag us down to say hello to Holly. I've brought most of them around to the bakery and she comes to my night skates in the evenings after closing up shop.

Her cheeks turn pink every time I compliment her proudly.

We lose track of Layla when she goes for another drink. I scan the party, seeing her talking to Theo at the bar.

"Want to dance?" I ask Holly once we're alone.

"Yes! But first..."

She hands me her cocktail and rifles through her

purse, squinting in the low light. I set our drinks on a table and hold her bag, shining my phone inside to make it easier for her.

"Thanks. I got you a little something to celebrate tonight."

She bites her lip, failing to hide her smile as she tucks the mystery gift behind her back in one hand. I lean around her to peek and she playfully keeps it out of sight.

"Yeah? You had so much faith in us winning? Shit, good thing we won."

"Haven't you heard? My guy, sixty-eight? He's a total beast on the ice."

Warmth fills my chest. "Your guy, huh?"

"All mine." She beams.

I knead her waist and taste her smile, claiming her mouth in a hungry kiss. She giggles into it. While I have her distracted, I catch her hand, feeling something small and smooth.

"Here."

Holly places a little snow globe in my hand. My smile spreads slowly when I see it's hockey themed. After I gave her a snow globe for Christmas, we've started buying them for each other all the time.

A delighted puff of laughter escapes me as I hold it up. The hockey player inside is wearing Mavs blue and my number. He's dipping his girl with pink hair and a bow in a kiss on an ice rink. The confetti snowflakes flip between white and yellow.

"Isn't it cute? I had it customized to include us in it together," she explains.

"It's unreal how happy you make me every day, sugar." I pull her into a bear hug.

Her sweet laughter is everything to me. I love hearing it and never want to go a day without it.

We've got a lifetime to look forward to—together.

Hugging her tighter, I lift my girl off her feet and carry her to the dance floor. I'm ready for all of it as long as I'm always with her.

Thank you so much for reading SAY IT ISN'T SNOW! If you can't get enough swoony hockey players, enjoy a free bonus scene of Holly and Caleb.

Download a free bonus scene:
bit.ly/vebonuscontent

Ready for more hockey heartthrobs to make you melt? Find out what happens when the coach's daughter gets a dating app match with her brother's best friend—and *her dad's new assistant coach* in MATCHING ALL THE WAY. Find all the books in the Heston U Hotshots series below.

Read MATCHING ALL THE WAY now:
veronicaedenauthor.com/hestonu

I WANT TO BE IN *every snow globe with you,* AS LONG AS WE'RE *together.*

BONUS DELETED SCENE

If you can't get enough of Caleb and Holly, enjoy a free bonus scene! Additional bonus content is available on my website. Visit the address below or scan the QR code to collect all available bonus content.

BONUS CONTENT:
www.veronicaedenauthor.com/bonus-content

ABOUT THE AUTHOR
STAY UP ALL NIGHT FALLING IN LOVE

Veronica Eden is a USA Today, Amazon Top 30, and International bestselling author of addictive romances that keep you up all night falling in love with spitfire heroines, and irresistible heroes.

She writes spicy contemporary romance and loves exploring the bond of characters that embrace *us against the world*. She's a fan of strong heroines and collecting as many book boyfriends as possible from swoony *"sin*namon rolls" with devastating smirks to gruff bad boys. When not writing, she can be found soaking up sunshine at the beach in Northeast Florida, snuggling in a pile with her untamed pack of animals (her husband, dog and cats), and surrounding herself with as many plants as she can get her hands on.

CONTACT + FOLLOW

Email: veronicaedenauthor@gmail.com
Website: http://veronicaedenauthor.com
FB Reader Group: bit.ly/veronicafbgroup
Amazon: amazon.com/author/veronicaeden

facebook.com/veronicaedenauthor

instagram.com/veronicaedenauthor

pinterest.com/veronicaedenauthor

bookbub.com/profile/veronica-eden

goodreads.com/veronicaedenauthor

ALSO BY VERONICA EDEN

Sign up for the mailing list to get first access and ARC opportunitics! **Follow Veronica on BookBub** for new release alerts!

New Adult Romance

Heston U Hotshots Series

Iced Out

Trick Play

Matching All the Way

Sinners and Saints Series

Wicked Saint

Tempting Devil

Ruthless Bishop

Savage Wilder

Sinners and Saints: The Complete Series

Crowned Crows Series

Crowned Crows of Thorne Point

Loyalty in the Shadows

A Fractured Reign

Printed in Dunstable, United Kingdom

71506525R00160